"Someda[y] [Your] Sassy Attitude's Gonna Get You Into Trouble," Deke Warned.

"I'm scared." It was obvious she wasn't.

His gaze ran intimately over her. "You should be."

Mary Beth watched him storm from the room. What on earth was wrong with her? All she had to do was bide her time, thank Deke for everything he'd helped with and watch him walk out of her life the way he'd done so easily two years ago. But no. She couldn't do that. Instead, she'd gone out of her way to provoke him.

It just wasn't in her nature to let another man run roughshod over her. She'd had enough of that from her father. She no longer had to listen to anyone tell her what she could or couldn't do.

Especially Deke.

Dear Reader,

'Tis the season to read six passionate, powerful and provocative love stories from Silhouette Desire!

Savor *A Cowboy & a Gentleman* (#1477), December's MAN OF THE MONTH, by beloved author Ann Major. A lonesome cowboy rekindles an old flame in this final title of our MAN OF THE MONTH promotion. MAN OF THE MONTH has had a memorable fourteen-year run and now it's time to make room for other exciting innovations, such as DYNASTIES: THE BARONES, a Boston-based Romeo-and-Juliet continuity with a happy ending, which launches next month, and—starting in June 2003—Desire's three-book sequel to Silhouette's out-of-series continuity THE LONE STAR COUNTRY CLUB. Desire's popular TEXAS CATTLEMAN'S CLUB continuity also returns in 2003, beginning in November.

This month DYNASTIES: THE CONNELLYS concludes with *Cherokee Marriage Dare* (#1478) by Sheri WhiteFeather, a riveting tale featuring a former Green Beret who rescues the youngest Connelly daughter from kidnappers. Award-winning, bestselling romance novelist Rochelle Alers debuts in Desire with *A Younger Man* (#1479), the compelling story of a widow's sensual renaissance. Barbara McCauley's *Royally Pregnant* (#1480) offers a fabulous finale to Silhouette's cross-line CROWN AND GLORY series, while a feisty rancher corrals the sexy cowboy-next-door in *Her Texas Temptation* (#1481) by Shirley Rogers. And a blizzard forces a lone wolf to deliver his hometown sweetheart's infant in *Baby & the Beast* (#1482) by Laura Wright.

Here's hoping you find all six of these supersensual Silhouette Desire titles in your Christmas stocking.

Enjoy!

Joan Marlow Golan

Joan Marlow Golan
Senior Editor, Silhouette Desire

Please address questions and book requests to:
Silhouette Reader Service
U.S.: 3010 Walden Ave., P.O. Box 1325, Buffalo, NY 14269
Canadian: P.O. Box 609, Fort Erie, Ont. L2A 5X3

Her Texan
Temptation
SHIRLEY ROGERS

Published by Silhouette Books
America's Publisher of Contemporary Romance

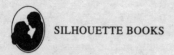

SILHOUETTE BOOKS

ISBN 0-373-76481-2

HER TEXAN TEMPTATION

Visit Silhouette at www.eHarlequin.com

Printed in U.S.A.

Books by Shirley Rogers

Silhouette Desire

Cowboys, Babies and Shotgun Vows #1176
Conveniently His #1266
A Cowboy, a Bride & a Wedding Vow #1344
Baby of Fortune #1384
One Wedding Night... #1434
Her Texan Temptation #1481

SHIRLEY ROGERS

lives in Virginia with her husband, two cats and an adorable Maltese named Blanca. She has two grown children, a son and a daughter. As a child, she was known for having a vivid imagination. It wasn't until she started reading romances that she realized her true destiny was writing them! Besides reading, she enjoys traveling, seeing movies and spending time with her family.

To my husband, Roger

One

"**G**ot a problem there, Red?"

Deke McCall!

Mary Beth Adams froze, the toe of her worn brown boot wedged in the hole she'd just kicked in a water trough. Water trickled out of the deteriorated wooden box, forming a small, muddy pool at her feet.

Of all the people in the world she wouldn't have wanted to catch her in such a dilemma, this heart-stopping cowboy from her past was at the top of her list. She cursed her temper as the taillights of her one and only ranch hand's car disappeared in the distance. How could he just up and quit? Even if he'd gotten another job offer, she at least deserved some notice.

Gathering her pride, she turned toward Deke, causing her ankle to twist a little more. Pain sliced through it and up her calf, clear into her thigh. She gritted her teeth. "No,

I'm just fine,'' she retorted, annoyed that he'd called her by the childhood nickname she detested.

As if the two years since she'd seen him had never passed, a startling thrill tingled her spine. Unprepared for the onslaught of emotion, Mary Beth fought for a sense of control.

You're not the same woman you were two years ago, harboring a schoolgirl crush, willing to give him your heart.

But by the rapid pounding in her chest, her heart didn't seem to be listening.

Shoring up her courage, she looked at Deke. Apparently rodeoing agreed with him. His shoulders were infinitely broad, his arms even more muscular than she remembered. It shouldn't hurt so much to see him.

Finally, because she couldn't put it off any longer, she lifted her eyes and met his gaze. Sitting atop his horse and leaning back comfortably in his saddle, he grinned at her. Blond strands of hair poked out of his straw cowboy hat. Those gorgeous McCall blue eyes twinkled a little too merrily.

Damned if he didn't look sexy.

"Yeah?" Deke tipped up his hat and held back a chuckle. Taller than most women, with curves that could stop a man in his tracks, Mary Beth was a sight to see. Balancing on one foot, her arms out like wings, she was shaking her hips in a provocative way that made him remember what it had felt like to make love to her.

Though most of her red hair was clasped behind her head, untamed wisps fell in cute little ringlets around her face, making her look more like nineteen than twenty-five. The glare in her green eyes suggested that the flush on her cheeks stemmed from her embarrassment rather than the late-summer Texas sun.

Gone was the young woman he remembered with the quiet, shy smile, the woman who'd seemed to blush modestly every time he'd spoken to her. Though they'd grown up in the same town, he'd been a couple of grades ahead of her. Truthfully he'd never paid much attention to Mary Beth.

Until that one night two years ago.

That one earth-shattering night had sent him a lethal warning that she could be a threat to his bachelorhood.

Shaking his head to clear his thoughts, he watched as she continued to wiggle her hips, trying his level best not to laugh outright. "Looks like you could use some help," he commented, his expression wry. A chuckle escaped his lips despite his best effort to contain himself.

"Thank you, but, no, I don't." What she needed was a miracle. A couple more months of problems that never seemed to let her get a step ahead, and she wouldn't have to worry about the note coming due on the ranch at all. Short of a miracle, Paradise would be owned by the bank.

And Mary Beth no longer believed in miracles.

With an air of dignity, she managed to work her foot out of the trough without falling and making a bigger fool of herself. Water gushed from the gaping hole. She quickly sidestepped it, then clamped her teeth together when she felt a sharp, stabbing pain in her right foot. Unable to put weight on it without adding to the biting pain, she lifted it slightly off the ground, shifting most of her weight to her other foot. "What are you doing here?" she demanded.

But even as she asked the question, her mind slipped back two years. Alone and hurting after her father's funeral, Deke had offered her comfort. It had been so easy to sink against him, to lose herself in his embrace. Though all of her life he'd barely noticed her, she'd been half in love with him since she'd been a teenager.

"Here in Texas or here on Paradise?" Deke asked, referring to her ranch.

Mary Beth looked around her, seeing the run-down ranch through his eyes. The disrepair of the house and outbuildings were obvious…and embarrassing. Even with the few head of cattle she ran, to call Paradise a ranch was a gross exaggeration. He was probably wondering why she'd let it get so dilapidated.

"On my land." She didn't care why he was back in Texas. Really, she didn't. He'd broken her heart. Maybe not intentionally. He hadn't *known* she'd harbored feelings for him all those years. But she'd suffered the sting of his rejection just the same. Well, times had changed. *She'd* changed. She was no longer a lovesick young girl, and she wouldn't be so susceptible to his charm again.

In her gut she'd known that a McCall would never take up with an Adams. At least, not permanently. Her family had been poor, while the McCalls owned the most profitable ranch in Crockett County. She shouldn't have been surprised when, after they'd made love, Deke had never bothered to call. But that hadn't made his leaving hurt any less.

Her curt tone caused his eyes to lose a bit of their sparkle. "Some of the cattle with your brand have broken through a fence, and I came over to investigate. Thought I'd better ride down here and let you know."

"I'll take care of it right away." How, she didn't know. Though undependable and trifling, Clyde, her ranch hand, had been better than nothing. Now he'd quit to take a job with a spread near Dallas. Great. Another man in her life who couldn't be depended on. When was she going to learn? With Clyde gone and without the money to hire anyone decent to replace him, she was on her own.

Why had she been obsessed with keeping this place?

What made her even think she wanted to try to make it turn a profit?

Because your father didn't think you have what it takes.

But her father had been dead two years now, and things on Paradise were worse instead of better. What was she doing here, still trying to prove a dead man wrong? If she had any sense, she'd quit and go back to her life in San Antonio.

Except, if she left now, she'd be the failure he'd always claimed she would be. She choked back a tear. Why couldn't he have loved her? If she'd been a son, his love and approval would have been automatic. But not for a girl.

Not for her.

"You expect Clyde back soon?"

Mary Beth blinked, her eyes focusing once again on her current problem—Deke McCall. "I said I'll take care of it," she said, ignoring his question. She'd figure a way to get the cattle off McCall land somehow. Damn, she hated asking for help. But the mortgage on the ranch was coming due, and if she lost even one head of cattle before she could sell them, she wasn't going to be able to meet the payment. Still, she'd risk even that before she'd stoop to asking Deke for anything.

Deke's eyebrows drew together as he sat up straight, his back rigid. "I just thought you might want me to lend a hand." He figured he deserved her ire. Years ago he'd taken advantage of her, had made love to her, then he'd left and hadn't so much as called her in the two years since. Now he'd shown up unexpectedly. What did he expect, a warm welcome?

He hadn't *planned* to make love to her.

She'd been gone from Crockett a couple of years. He'd heard she'd been living in San Antonio. Then she'd been

called home because her father had been in an accident.
Hank Adams had passed away a couple of weeks after
she'd arrived at Paradise.

Out of respect Deke had attended the funeral. He hadn't
cared much for Hank, but then, not many people had. Mary
Beth had caught Deke's attention when he'd spotted her
in the crowd of well-wishers gathered around her. She'd
returned to Crockett a changed woman, confident and vi-
vacious, with a smile and a good word—for everyone, it
seemed, but him.

That's why he'd lingered at her house after the funeral
when everyone one else had left. It had bothered him when
he'd sensed that she had gone out of her way to avoid him.

"Thanks, anyway." Mary Beth shook her head. A warm
September breeze caught a strand of her hair, and she
brushed it from her face. "If that's all—"

Her brusque tone sent Deke a distinct message—she
didn't want him hanging around. He was downright of-
fended and actually considered leaving. But since Clyde
wasn't there, Deke had a niggling doubt about her assurance that she could get the cattle rounded up. Whether she
wanted to admit it or not, she needed his help. Despite the
fact that she wanted to be rid of him, he couldn't leave
her in a jam. Hell, the neighborly thing to do would be to
lend her a hand.

"Look," he began calmly, "I can help you round up
the strays. We can have it done in no time, then I'll leave
you alone."

Mary Beth lifted her chin. "I don't need your help."
Feeling light-headed, she put her hand to her forehead,
which was damp from sweat. Either the sun was getting
to her, or her injury was worse than she'd thought. If she
didn't do something soon for the pain and swelling in her
ankle, she was going to faint right in front of him!

Deke looked skyward and frowned at the churn of black clouds. "Looks like a storm's brewing. With both of us working, we can probably beat the rain." His gaze turned to Mary Beth again. A familiar longing that he'd thought he'd overcome stirred in his chest. After making love with her, he'd lain there stunned…and wanting more. But what she'd made him feel, what she'd made him long for, went way past physical need. If he wasn't careful, a relationship with a woman like her could lead to more, much more than he had to give.

Apparently he'd been right, if she could affect him so easily after all this time.

"I wouldn't want to keep you from something important," she said with as much aloofness as she could muster. "Aren't you suppose to be at a rodeo or something?" Because she couldn't stand on one leg much longer, she put her foot down. A stinging sensation stole her breath, but she remained still, determined not to give him a reason to stay.

Noting a trace of disdain in her voice, Deke's lips thinned. "I've been home on a short break." Did she dislike rodeo cowboys in general or him in particular? Before she could conceal it, he caught the look of anguish that flashed through her eyes. He quickly swung his leg over his horse and dismounted, annoyed that he hadn't realized she was injured. In an instant he was by her side. "What'd you do? Hurt yourself?" Frowning, he knelt on one knee and touched her leg.

"Get your hands off me!" she blurted, then shoved his shoulder hard.

Already down on his haunches, Deke braced his hand on the ground, barely stopping himself from falling on his backside. He shot her a hard look. "Calm down," he commanded. Using his other hand, he clasped her thigh just above her knee. "I'm just gonna check your foot."

"My *foot* is fine." She wasn't lying. It was her ankle that was killing her. But Deke didn't have to know that.

He ignored her. As long as he'd known her, Mary Beth had never wanted to accept a helping hand. She was unlike her father in that way. Hank Adams, in Deke's opinion, had always been looking for the easy way in life, while Mary Beth had diligently taken care of her sick mother, as well as the cooking, cleaning and whatever else it took to make her mother's life easier. He couldn't help thinking that Mary Beth was going to spend her life trying to live down her father's irresponsible reputation.

Turning his attention to her injury, Deke carefully lifted her leg and propped it on his thigh. To maintain her balance, Mary Beth touched the tips of her fingers to his shoulder. His gut tightened from the contact, and he tried not to notice her light scent. As he gingerly worked off her boot, Deke remembered the last time he'd undressed her.

That evening he'd only meant to console her. It seemed as if she'd been holding herself in check all day. Finally, alone with him, everything crashed in on her. She'd crumbled against him and confided that with her father's death, she'd felt all alone. And she'd missed her mother, who had died only a year before.

Deke had held her and whispered words of comfort. When she'd looked at him, her eyes filled with tears, he'd kissed them away, soothing her sorrow. Mary Beth had burrowed closer, pressing herself to him, and Deke had given in to a need to taste her. Their kisses had quickly ignited a fire between them that soon raged out of control. Not wanting to take advantage of her momentary weakness, he'd tried to hold back. But she'd pulled him to her and whispered that she'd needed him.

Caught in a delicate moment between compassion and desire, he'd made love to her.

A mistake.

No.

A *big* mistake.

He'd made a quick retreat, leaving before she could get under his skin. Or so he'd thought. Later, alone in his room, he'd discovered he hadn't left quick enough. Being with Mary Beth that night had touched something deep inside him. Shamefully, he hadn't called her because she'd have wanted promises—promises he wouldn't have been able to give.

Then or now.

"Stay still," he ordered brusquely, annoyed that he'd let his thoughts drift into forbidden territory. Again. He had to get out of there before he went crazy with wanting her. But he couldn't leave her injured. He'd hang around long enough to see that she was okay. Then he'd be out like a shot—away from her. Because with her this close, she was a threat to him, to everything he'd been working for on the rodeo circuit.

He couldn't stay. And he sure as hell didn't want to hurt her again.

"I can't, with you holding on to my leg." She tried not to fall on her butt. She didn't like being this close to him, didn't want to feel his heat. Touching him provoked memories she'd tried to forget. However, she was no longer the innocent girl she'd been two years ago. Back then she'd been so unbelievably needy, wanting him to see her as a woman. Of course, he probably hadn't even thought about her since that night.

Sensitive to his touch, she felt as if the warmth of his

hands scored her skin as he pulled off her sock and exposed her swollen ankle. Mary Beth's breath caught, but it wasn't from pain. She remembered how it had felt when he'd used those same hands to intimately caress her body.

Don't do this! Don't let him near your heart again!

When she looked at him, she wondered if she'd spoken aloud. Deke's blue eyes were studying her in a way that made her feel naked. The fist in her chest squeezed a little tighter, making it difficult to breathe. Then she realized that *he* was speaking to *her*.

"Sweetheart, how bad does it hurt?" he asked again, looking away to examine the injury more closely.

"Only a little," she answered, but her teeth clenched as he gently rotated her ankle, checking to see if she'd broken a bone.

His gaze sliced back to her, and he arched a brow. "Liar."

Damn. Mary Beth felt her cheeks burn. Lord, she hated the way she turned all red when embarrassed or angry. "If you'll just let me go, I'll be fine. All I have to do is put my boot back on, and I'll—"

"The only thing you're gonna do is put some ice on this," Deke told her firmly.

Mary Beth bristled. His advice sounded more like an order. She jerked her foot from his hold on it, cursing in agony under her breath. The last thing she wanted was advice from the man who had trampled her heart. "Look, I don't need you to tell me what to do."

Deke stood and planted his hands on his hips. "Obviously, you need someone to, if you think you're gonna be able to put your boot back on."

At six foot, he was only about four inches taller than her, but the determination on his face and his effect on her senses made his presence seem overwhelming. Mary Beth braced herself as best she could and took a cautious step away, then clamped her lips together to bear a sharp, stabbing sensation in her leg. "I have things to do. I can't sit around and nurse a little bruise." Even as she said the words, her face contorted.

He gave her a dark glare. "Let Clyde do them when he gets back." Deke reached down and retrieved her sock and boot, but instead of handing them back to her, he held on to them.

Mary Beth's heartbeat quickened. She didn't want to admit that Clyde had left for good. Why couldn't Deke have gone when she'd first asked him? Until now, she'd been able to handle things at the ranch—barely. Now he'd walked in to mess with her heart. Well, she wasn't going to take it. As far as she was concerned, he could just mount up and ride off.

Except, as much as she wanted to tell him to get lost, she really had little choice but to admit that Clyde had quit. The whole town of Crockett would soon find out that the no-account jerk had left. When Deke heard about it, he'd come back madder than a raging bull because she hadn't told him.

Taking a deep breath, she admitted, "I can't."

"Why not?" Deke glanced up the road as if he would see a cloud of dust from Clyde's car, then he looked back at her. "How long will he be gone?"

"Forever," she grated. "He quit."

"Just now?"

She gave a slight nod. "He took a job near Dallas."

"Ah, so that's why you were throwing a tantrum," Deke concluded, a hint of a smile playing on his lips.

"Oh, give me my boot," she practically snarled, trying to snatch it from him. His easy grin made her heart trip over itself. She'd known Deke for many years, had seen his effect on females of all ages. He had the power to charm a raw steak from a starving dog. She stiffened her spine, refusing to be such an easy target again.

Deke held her boot captive, just out of her reach. "Knock it off, Red."

Mary Beth's eyes blazed. "Stop calling me that!"

"What? Red?" he asked, his tone mystified. "Hell, sweetheart, you've been known by that nickname for as long as I can remember."

"I don't like it. I never have. I go by Mary Beth!" she snapped. Maybe she sounded petulant, but at this moment she damn well didn't care. She'd been teased about her hair since she'd entered elementary school because it had been the color of a raging fire. Some of the kids had taunted her mercilessly when she'd revealed her dislike of that awful nickname. When she'd moved to San Antonio, she'd used Mary Beth as her name. She sure didn't want Deke calling her Red, especially since her hair had turned to a rich shade of cinnamon.

"Well, I'll sure try to remember that, Mary Beth," Deke replied, emphasizing her name. He frowned. It seemed that he couldn't say anything right. He hadn't seen much of her in the past two years, and the times he had, she'd avoided him. Damn, she hadn't even spoken to him.

But in all fairness to her, he couldn't have stayed with her and been the man she needed. Like her he'd lost his father. Though it had been years ago, Deke still carried the weight of the last words he'd spoken to him.

"I hate you."

Poorly chosen words by a boy, haunting words for the man he'd become. Words he could never take back. He'd learned his lesson the hard way, learned not to say something he didn't mean.

And that's why he hadn't called Mary Beth after they'd

made love. He hadn't wanted to give her false hope, dreams he couldn't fulfill. And in his effort to be altruistic, he'd hurt her.

Shaking off the bad memories, Deke turned his attention back to her ankle, now swollen even more and turning pink. "Look, you've got to treat that right now, or you're not going to be walking on it for at least a week."

"Well, thank you, Dr. McCall, for your advice."

Her icy reply made Deke flinch. He stared at her, half expecting to see frostbite forming on her lips. Instead they were as full and tempting as the last time he'd kissed them. He could still remember her taste. "I'm serious," he grated, trying to direct his mind back to her injury and away from his smoldering lust.

"I don't have time to argue with you. I've got cattle to round up," she reminded him. Mary Beth tried to nab her boot from him, but he quickly held it out of her reach.

A muscle worked along his jaw. "They're not going far."

"That isn't the point. They're certainly not going to come home if I whistle for them, now are they?"

"You've got a smart mouth," Deke growled, and his gaze slid to her lips. He couldn't stop himself from thinking of how it would feel to kiss them again.

Whoa, don't go there. That kind of thinking is what got you into bed with Mary Beth the last time.

She tried to grab her boot again. "Give it here!"

"If you keep that up, I'm gonna think you don't want me here."

"Now that you mention it—"

"Careful, sweetheart, or you're going to hurt my feelings," he drawled.

"As if I could," Mary Beth muttered. She glowered at him. "Are you through now? I've got work to do."

"It can wait. Come on, I'll get you into the house, and we'll put some ice on your ankle."

"Deke—"

"Dammit, Mary Beth—" Deke stopped talking and swept her up in his arms, dropping her boot and sock in the process. He hadn't remembered her being so stubborn!

"Deke McCall, put me down this minute!" Her demand was met with a silencing stare. She kicked her legs and pushed at his chest with her hand. "I can walk!"

He shook his head. "Not without causing more damage to your ankle. And stop fighting me, or I'm gonna drop you." To add credibility to his warning, he allowed her to slip a little in his arms. She squealed, then her arms flew around his neck and she held on tight. Deke felt the brush of one breast against his chest, and a burning sensation ignited in his gut.

Damn! Just how long could it take him to walk to her house?

He covered the distance to her door in deliberate, long strides, then took the three steps to the small porch as one, tightening his arms around her to keep from dropping her as he opened the door. Despite the air-conditioning cooling his skin as he walked inside, his body felt as if it was in flames. Grimacing, he shoved the door closed with his shoulder.

Memories assailed him as his eyes adjusted to the dim light inside the house. He looked at Mary Beth, and he knew she was thinking the same thing.

The last time he'd been here, they'd made love.

Hell.

He was in trouble.

Two

As Deke strode through the foyer, he tried to force thoughts of Mary Beth naked and writhing beneath him from his mind.

It didn't work.

Sweat beaded his brow. Knowing he wasn't the right man for her, that he could never be the man she needed, should have been enough to make him keep his hands off her.

But he hadn't. He'd made love to her, and like the bastard he was, he'd walked away.

Hell. All he was good at was hurting people. Mary Beth didn't need anyone to hurt her. She needed someone she could count on, not a footloose cowboy whose only goal in life was to win the National Finals Rodeo bull-riding championship.

He could have gone to see her later, or at least called her. He could have apologized. But he hadn't. Figuring

Mary Beth was the kind of woman who was looking for marriage and happily-ever-after, he'd decided the best thing to do was to make a clean break.

If you'd gone to see her, you might not have been able to walk away. And that's what had scared him the most. He couldn't have stayed and given her what she needed. He'd had his own agenda. He *had* to win the championship.

For his father.

Jacob McCall had gone to his grave thinking that his son hated him, and Deke had lived every single day knowing how much he'd let his father down, knowing it was too late to tell his father how very sorry he was. It gnawed at his gut, tearing him up inside. He'd learned his lesson the hard way, and he would never make that mistake again.

Deke had only himself to blame. At fifteen, he'd had it all figured out. He'd had plans with Becky Parsons to go to the lake, where they were going to finally get past the heavy petting they'd been enjoying and get down to some hot-and-heavy sex. Deke was anxious to lose his virginity, and Becky had been more than willing to let him take hers.

But earlier that day his father had grounded him because he'd been ignoring his chores, and his grades had begun to slip. Usually, Deke had been able to cajole his father into giving him another chance, but this time his dad hadn't budged. Deke had been furious. All he could think about was meeting Becky. So he'd sneaked out. When Jacob McCall had discovered his son missing, he'd come after him and hauled him home. Angry and embarrassed, Deke had said some terrible things to his father.

"I hate you."

The next day, Deke had held on to his anger when his parents were leaving on a trip. He'd hugged his mother goodbye, but had refused to speak to his father. His parents had been killed later that day when the plane his father was piloting developed engine trouble and crashed. Deke had never had the opportunity to make amends. He'd never had the chance to take those hateful words back—to tell his father that he didn't mean them, that he loved him.

After the funeral, standing over his father's grave, he'd promised to make it up to him. Together they'd shared an interest in the rodeo, and his father had indulged Deke's desire to participate. Now all Deke wanted was to win the championship bull-riding event for his father.

Currently, he was the front-runner, and he wasn't going to let anything or anyone, including Mary Beth, get in the way of that goal. He'd made a lot of mistakes in his life, but this time he was going to do the right thing.

"Okay, we're inside now so put me down!" Mary Beth demanded, interrupting his thoughts.

"In a minute." Deke continued down the hallway until he came to the kitchen. He used his boot to drag a wooden chair from under the table, then with great care he deposited Mary Beth on it. Her hands slid down his chest as she eased her arms from around his neck.

Damn! It was a mistake to be here with her. He straightened and looked down at her, his heart beating hard and fast. Mary Beth started to get up, but he put his hand firmly on her shoulder, effectively keeping her in place.

"Sit still," he ordered gruffly. Without speaking, she brooded, her arms crossed in front of her voluptuous chest, her bottom lip stuck out in a pout.

Irritated by the entire situation, he grabbed hold of another kitchen chair. As he pulled it away from the table, a large stack of magazines slid off it and fell to the floor. "Sorry," he muttered, then bent down and began gathering them.

"It's okay," she replied, watching him, and her cheeks reddened slightly.

Deke continued stacking them together, noticing that they were dated and worn. The one that ended up on the top of the pile had a picturesque location easily identified as Paris, France, by the Eiffel Tower. He picked up the magazines and straightened them, then put the pile on the table.

Grabbing the chair again, he positioned it in front of her, then carefully elevated her leg.

"I have to see to the cattle," she stated when she could no longer hold her silence.

"I'll make sure they're taken care of," Deke assured her. "But first, we need to do something to get that swelling down. Stay put." His threatening look dared her to disobey.

"This is ridiculous." Mary Beth examined her ankle. "It's not that bad." Still, she didn't get up. "Besides, I don't have to be on my ankle to round up cattle."

"What if you have to get off your horse?"

"It won't hurt me to walk on it for a little while."

"Yes, it will. I don't think your ankle's broken, but it might be a good idea to get it x-rayed."

Mary Beth mentally reviewed her dwindling bank account. A visit to the doctor would cost precious money she didn't have to spare. "I don't need it x-rayed. It's just a sprain."

"Well, I've had a lot of sprains, and I've learned enough about treating them to know that the first twenty-four hours are the most important. If you don't get the swelling down, it'll take even longer for it to heal."

She huffed. Deke ignored her and started opening and closing the drawers in the kitchen cabinets. Mary Beth looked around the dismal room and cringed. A path was worn across the faded cream-colored vinyl floor, and at best the gas stove could be called a relic. The yellow-flowered curtains sewn by her mother years ago were shabby, bleached by constant morning sun. Mary Beth could still remember the day she'd helped her mother hang them. Sadly, it was the last thing Della Adams had ever done before she'd taken ill.

Having just graduated high school, Mary Beth had set her sights on leaving Crockett. It was a blow to her plans when her mother had become sick. Mary Beth stayed home to care for her, and it had been months before the doctors had discovered her cancer. Della had fought the terrible disease for six years. They'd driven countless times to San Antonio, then later to San Luis once the new hospital had opened.

But the cancer had continued to spread, leaving her mother with little energy to fight it. And when she'd lost her mother, Mary Beth had lost her best friend.

What must Deke be thinking? she wondered. Her cheeks colored slightly as she sat in the dumpy room watching him. His family's ranch, the Bar M, was large and prosperous, a far cry from the failing acres of Paradise.

Because her days were now spent trying to care for the livestock and the land, Mary Beth hadn't had the time, or the money for that matter, to fix up the inside of the house. She done her best to tidy the small place when she'd first returned home, but sparing the time had been difficult. Nowadays, she rarely had energy at the end of the day to do more than pick up behind herself.

Hearing that her father had been hurt after being thrown from his horse, Mary Beth had made arrangements to take a leave from her job and come home and help him. Upon arriving, she'd learned that he'd broken several ribs and his leg. One of his ribs had punctured a lung, and because his health was poor, he'd developed pneumonia. Unable to fight it off, Hank Adams had died shortly after she'd arrived.

The slamming of yet another drawer drew her attention. Mary Beth found herself watching Deke's rear end as he moved around the room. His worn jeans encased his butt in a tight, all-too-appealing fit. She gritted her teeth, hating that he still had an effect on her.

"What are you looking for?" she demanded when he continued to peruse her cabinet drawers. His quick movements were maddening when she just wanted him gone.

"A cloth or something to put some ice in."

"They're over there." She pointed to a drawer across the room.

Deke looked in the direction she indicated, then walked over and yanked open the drawer. "This'll do." He pulled out a frayed white dishcloth with multicolored stripes, crossed the room to the old refrigerator and opened the freezer door. Reaching inside, he took some ice, gathered it in the cloth, then spread it on the counter and methodically adjusted the cubes, folding them inside.

"Here you go," he said as he approached her.

She waited for him to put the ice on her ankle, then caught her breath when the cold compress touched her skin. The weight of it made her ankle ache even more.

"How does that feel?"

She glared at him. "Cold."

He nodded. "Yeah, well, that's how it's supposed to feel." Deke let go and stepped back, pleased with his work.

The ice pack fell to the side.

Frowning, he picked it up and put it back on. Before he could move away, it fell off again. "Damn," he muttered.

"I can hold it," she told him, and reached for the compress.

"Yeah? How? You can't lean over and hold it on there for very long. Your back'll be sore after a while." Before she could protest, he gave her the ice pack, then lifted her and carried her toward the living room.

"Will you put me down?" Mary Beth rasped, her tone revealing her frustration.

"In a minute." He settled her on the sofa, then grabbed a small throw pillow and stuffed it under her foot. "I'll get you a more comfortable one from your bedroom in a minute," he told her. Taking the ice pack from her, he put it back on the sprain. This time, propped against the sofa, it stayed in place.

"This is fine." Mary Beth didn't want to think about Deke going anywhere near her bedroom. The last time he'd been in her house, he'd not only been in her bedroom, but in her bed.

And they'd made love.

Had sex, she corrected herself. For Deke it surely hadn't been anything more, as he'd proven when he'd walked out the next morning and never bothered to call her. He'd probably felt sorry for her because her father had just died. Undoubtedly, he'd been just as surprised as she was when he'd kissed her. When she'd returned his kisses, well, she supposed he was used to women offering him sex.

It hadn't been that way for her. The crush on him she'd nurtured as a teenager had resurfaced when Deke had taken her in his arms, when he'd kissed her. She'd always wondered what it would be like to be intimate with him.

And the instant his lips had touched hers, she'd known that she couldn't deny herself the pleasure of finding out. She'd waited a long time for Deke McCall to notice her.

And making love with him had been…incredible. Everything she'd dreamed it would be.

His voice interrupted her thoughts, and she gave him a blank look. "What?"

"I said, now that you've got ice on it, how about something for the pain?" he repeated, his tone a shade more tolerant than a minute ago.

"I'm sure there's something in the kitchen or bathroom, but don't worry about it. I'll take something later," she said, unwilling to admit that her ankle was throbbing. And on top of everything else, her head felt as if someone was pounding on it with a large rock. The thought of Deke prowling through her personal belongings made it feel a thousand times worse.

"You need to take something now."

She sat forward, and her expression sobered. "I appreciate your help, but I can take care of myself. I'm used to doing it." Used to not depending on a man. Her father had taught her that lesson well, because he'd never been around when he was needed.

Deke's blue eyes sailed into hers. "Well, it won't hurt you to let someone else look after you for a change." She had a right to be angry with him. And he damned well didn't deserve her forgiveness. He wouldn't ask her for it because he could never make it up to her. But the least he could do before he left was to make sure she was okay. "I'll see to the horses, then I'll find something for you to take for the pain."

Without waiting for her to answer, Deke went outside. He made short work of unsaddling the horses, then returned to the house. As he searched the kitchen cabinets for some medicine, he noticed the walls were badly in need of a fresh coat of paint, and the floor looked as if it was a lot older than his twenty-eight years.

Deke figured that the house was easily over seventy years old, and sadly, it showed. Mary Beth's father sure hadn't taken much interest in keeping the place up. Shaking his head, Deke thought the entire ranch needed a dreadful amount of work before it would begin to look decent. The barn was missing shingles, and the machine shed desperately needed a new coat of paint.

He'd only been home for a short break from the rodeo, but that had been long enough to hear the rumors of Mary Beth's struggles to keep the ranch afloat since her father's death. And now her only ranch hand had quit. How was she going to manage alone—especially since she'd injured her ankle?

Logically Deke knew Mary Beth's problems shouldn't concern him, but he couldn't help thinking about how hard it was going to be for her. She needed help. And, after all, he was her neighbor. Maybe lending her a hand would go a long way toward making amends for treating her so badly.

Remembering the stray cattle that still needed tending, as he continued to poke through her cabinets, he grabbed the phone receiver off the wall. His sister-in-law, Ashley, who was married to Ryder, answered on the third ring. Deke asked her to let one of his brothers, Ryder or Jake, know about the strays and the fencing so they could get someone out there to handle the problem. Then he explained that Mary Beth had hurt herself, and he was going to hang around awhile to be sure she was okay.

That done and unable to find any medicine, Deke left the kitchen and headed toward the bathroom. A quick search of the old wooden cabinet in the bathroom turned up a bottle of over-the-counter medicine. He filled a glass sitting on the side of the sink with water, then went in search of a couple of pillows to make her more comfortable.

As he walked down the narrow hallway, he noticed that all of the bedroom doors were shut. He started to go into what he remembered as Mary Beth's room, but instead turned toward the room her father had used, figuring she'd moved into the larger room after his death. As soon as he stepped inside, he halted in his tracks.

The musty, unused smell hit him as he scanned the room. The faded, drawn curtains filtered a smattering of light from the late-afternoon sun. He flipped the switch, bathing the room in soft light from a ceiling fixture covered by a square of milky-white glass.

The room was clean and tidy. A little *too* neat. The closet door was shut, the bed undisturbed. Still, something didn't quite seem right.

Then he saw them. A pair of man's shoes in the corner of the room.

Deke's heart stopped. Did Mary Beth have a man living with her? No, that didn't make sense. If a man was living here, where was he? *Who* was he? Irritation at someone sharing her bed, however illogical, twisted his gut. Then he paused.

If she was living with someone, he would have heard about it for sure. Old Mrs. Weaver, Crockett's worst gossip, would have made sure the entire town knew about it.

Deke sniffed the stale air. Curious, he moved farther into the room. A man's gold wristwatch rested on a wooden tray on the dresser, along with a small amount of change and a large pocket knife. He frowned as he studied the articles.

Opening the closet door, Deke found it half-full of a man's clothes. The floor of the closet was filled with boxes and shoes. The shelf above held more boxes. What the hell was going on? He checked the dresser drawers, and most of them held piles of neatly folded shirts and pants, tainted with the fragrance of time. In the adjoining bathroom, he discovered more unsettling clues. Though clean, it looked undisturbed. An array of shaving lotion and cologne covered almost one whole side of the small countertop. A toothbrush hung in a rusting metal fixture.

Then he realized that the room hadn't been touched since Mary Beth's father had died.

Deke was dumbfounded.

She's still grieving for Hank, he thought.

Feeling empathy, he could understand, because he was still dealing with his own demons concerning his relationship with his father. The fight they'd had haunted him. He would take every word back if it was in his power. But that time was long lost.

Shaking his head, Deke didn't think it was a good sign that Mary Beth was hanging on to Hank's belongings. And it probably wasn't his place to mention it, but then again, if he didn't, who would? Mary Beth was all alone out here.

Still mulling over what he should do, he left the room, closing the door quietly behind him. He stepped across the hall and opened the door to Mary Beth's bedroom. As he walked inside, her unique womanly scent halted his movements. This room was also tidy, though the bed was unmade, as if she'd just climbed from it.

Deke stared at the rumpled bedding, and the memory of making love to Mary Beth right there on that bed caused his chest to ache. Why couldn't he forget what it felt like to make love to her? What was it about her that was so different from other women he'd known?

It had been good between him and Mary Beth. Too damn good. Good enough to scare the pants off him. He snatched two pillows from the bed. Tucking them under his arm, he went back to the living room. Mary Beth was scrunched down on the sofa, her head resting against the arm. She looked so damn vulnerable. So fragile.

She would probably laugh at that, he thought with sardonic amusement. He had a feeling that Mary Beth wouldn't appreciate him thinking of her as fragile in any way. Deke walked over and gently touched her shoulder.

"Oh," she murmured as she slowly opened her eyes.

When she appeared to gain her bearings, he handed her the glass of water. "Here, take these," he instructed softly, opening the medicine bottle.

She held out her hand, and he dropped two white pills in her palm. "Thank you." She popped the pills in her mouth, then drank some water. "There. Are you satisfied?"

Deke frowned as he placed one of the pillows behind her so she could rest easier. "I'm only trying to help." Despite her surly tone, he tried to make her more comfortable by sliding the other pillow under her foot.

Mary Beth looked repentant. Okay, so he *had* been helpful, and she should have expressed a little gratitude instead of being so disagreeable. "I know. I'm sorry."

Taking the glass from her, he set it beside yet another stack of old magazines on the table beside the sofa. He stared absently at them a moment, then turned his head to look at her. "I called the Bar M. Someone's going to round up your cattle and repair the hole in the fence. So you don't have to worry about anything."

Mary Beth cocked her head as she looked into his eyes. "I appreciate the help, Deke. Really. But your family's already done too much for me these past two years." She was relieved that the cattle were being seen to, but that the McCalls were handling the problem made her feel even more indebted to them. How could she ever repay their kindness?

Taking note of the worn fabric on the arms, Deke made himself comfortable in a chair across from her. "It's not a big deal, Mary Beth."

Her eyes fell away from his. "Yes, it is."

The problems at Paradise were becoming overwhelming, and the weight of her need to make the ranch successful was dragging her down. Though she was barely hanging on, she refused to depend on others to help her.

She had to prove her father wrong.

He'd never given her a chance to show him that she could help. It was a man's job, he'd told her more than once, with a harsh tone that revealed his disappointment in having a daughter and not a son.

"Not if you don't make it one."

Deke's soft reply interrupted her thoughts. Her gaze went to his again, and he smiled. Her stomach tingled, like tiny butterflies were having a party inside it. "I'm not trying to be difficult."

"Sure could've fooled me." His eyes stayed on hers.

"I appreciate everything you've done. I'm just not used to having someone around helping."

"Like your father?"

Mary Beth wanted to say no. She really did. But that wouldn't have been an honest answer. Her father had never been around when she and her mother had needed him. He'd only cared about money. Money he never seemed to have. Feeling her spirits fall, she tried to hold the bitter feelings at bay. "Yeah."

"I can understand how hard it's been."

She swallowed hard. Deke didn't know. No one had any idea that she held bitter feelings toward her father. Shamefully, she hadn't even wanted to come back when she'd heard he was ill. But if she hadn't, people would've talked. The lump that had lodged in her throat refused to move when she swallowed.

An awkward moment of silence filled the room. She looked at Deke, and his mouth quirked up at one corner. Mary Beth found the sight much too appealing. He started to speak, stopped himself as if considering his words, then sighed.

"What?"

He waited a moment, then asked, "Why haven't you cleaned out your father's things?"

She stilled. "What…what do you mean?"

"I wasn't snooping," he said quickly. "I was looking for some pillows, and I went into your father's bedroom, thinking that you'd made it your room since his death."

"You went into his room?"

He nodded. "I guess you've had a rough time."

"Losing my father, you mean?" She wasn't sure what to say. He was expecting her to tell him all about how she'd cried, how hard it had been to lose someone she'd loved. So hard that she hadn't been able to bring herself to go through his belongings.

She had felt grief. Not the unbearable kind she'd felt when her mother had died. But it had been grief, tempered with resentment and anger. Resentment because Hank Adams had never let her close to him, anger because he hadn't loved her.

"I just haven't had the time to finish it," she said quietly. "Taking care of the ranch has been a priority. His room and clothing can wait."

"It's been two years," Deke pointed out, his expression thoughtful. "You haven't had time in two years to go through his things?" He wasn't sure he believed her and sensed she was putting it off. He wondered why.

She looked away from his probing eyes. "I just said so, didn't I?"

"Don't get testy," Deke retorted, but his words came with another smile.

"I'm not."

"Are, too," he returned.

Mary Beth squeezed her eyes closed, fighting the sting of tears. She couldn't let Deke know how hard it had been for her to keep the ranch going. Her stupid idea of taking over and trying to make it a success was literally blowing up in her face. Very soon it was going to come crashing down around her.

More in control, she opened her eyes and looked at him. "Look, I really appreciate what you've done, but I'm tired and I'd like to rest." She glanced at her watch and was astonished at how much time had passed since Deke had arrived. "Besides, it's getting late, and I'm sure you have other things to do."

Instead of getting up, he settled himself more into the soft chair, sitting back comfortably and stretching his legs out in front of him. "I thought I'd hang around a while. You know, to make sure you're okay." Maybe he'd stay and make her something to eat for dinner.

Mary Beth yawned and leaned back against the pillow. She fought closing her eyes. "That's not necessary. I'll be fine now."

"Stop arguing and try to rest," Deke suggested.

"You don't need to stay," she murmured, and her eyelids drifted shut. She wanted him to leave. Maybe when he did, her pulse would go back to a normal beat. Having Deke McCall around was dangerous to her heart. He'd been nice to take care of her, but a part of her was still very attracted to him, and she didn't need the temptation of his hard, lean body or his charming smile.

Besides, he was only looking out for her because it was the neighborly thing to do.

As much as she might wish, Deke McCall wasn't her miracle.

Three

Mary Beth's cupboards left a lot to be desired.

Deke studied the choices before him. Canned soup, rice, a jar of spaghetti sauce, noodles and an array of canned vegetables. He'd already searched her freezer for some kind of meat to prepare, but considering he wasn't a great cook by any stretch of the imagination, he figured he'd better not get too creative.

He settled for the jar of spaghetti sauce and a box of macaroni in the shape of small shells. Adding the pasta to a pot of boiling water, he then poured the spaghetti sauce in a bowl and placed it inside a large microwave oven. It was so old that Deke figured the radiation it emitted could quite possibly make him sterile.

He wasn't sure what had prompted him to stay around to take care of Mary Beth, especially since she'd made it perfectly clear she didn't want his company.

Guilt.

Yeah, there was that, he told himself. He couldn't change what had happened between them in the past. All he could do was make sure he didn't hurt her again.

Lust.

Now his brain was getting to the heart of the matter, and his body reacted in kind, sending a surge of blood below his belt. Hell, he was still attracted to her. Just thinking about her lying on the couch made him dream things he had no business dreaming about.

Okay, get your mind back on cooking. Serve her dinner, make sure she's okay, then get the hell out before you do something you'll regret.

Like kiss her.

Oh, yeah, he was going to be in deep trouble if he couldn't keep his mind off kissing her. He'd stayed with her at first because he couldn't have left her alone to take care of herself. But now, after spending the afternoon watching over her, he'd found himself watching *her.*

Wanting her.

A hissing sound drew his attention. Realizing that the macaroni was boiling over, he turned down the heat and mopped up the mess. While the noodles finished cooking, he heated the sauce a little more, then searched for some kind of bread to go with the meal.

Finding none in her pantry, he walked to the refrigerator. As he started to open the door, a picture taped to the front of it caught his eye. Taken in the moonlight, the scene seemed so out of place in her dingy kitchen that it had almost jumped out at him.

Now the picture seemed to mesmerize him. "Mexico— Experience the Magic" was emblazoned bold-faced across the top of it. Amid the backdrop of the shimmering gulf and a magnificent full moon, two lovers lay on the sand, entwined in each other's arms.

Examining it, Deke noticed the serrated edges of the paper and suspected that it had been torn from one of the magazines. Was Mary Beth planning a vacation? She must be, he thought, remembering all the travel magazines he'd seen lying around.

But how could she be planning a trip? It didn't seem like something Mary Beth would do. She'd always been so level-headed. Surely she wouldn't spend money on a vacation when the ranch needed so much work.

Or would she? Did he really know her that well? Deke had to admit that he didn't. As kids, they'd never really been friends. To tell the truth, he'd always just thought of her as a neighbor.

But he'd thought about her a lot after they'd made love. Mainly that he wanted to make love with her again, and that had scared the living daylights out of him. Over the past two years, his views on getting involved with a woman hadn't changed. After seeing his two older brothers and his sister recently marry, Deke was wary of spending too much time with the same woman.

He was better off alone, where he wouldn't let down anyone he loved.

Like you let your father down.

Yeah, he should feel guilty, he told himself. Living with guilt made him steer clear of women with white lace and flowers on their mind.

Women like Mary Beth.

He ran his hand along the edge of the picture, then sighed and opened the refrigerator door. There was a can of biscuits on a shelf, and thinking a week or so wasn't too long, he ignored the purchase-by date and popped open the can. Within a few minutes they were baking in the oven.

With the rest of the meal ready, he put the full plates

on the table, filled glasses with tea he found already made in the fridge, then went to see if Mary Beth was still asleep.

She was. She'd shifted to her side on the sofa, and her short white T-shirt had bunched up, baring her midriff. His gaze ran slowly over her. Her skin looked smooth and satiny. Her jeans were snug on her hips, and his mind wandered to that tiny mole he remembered being right at the top of her thigh. He'd thought it kind of sexy.

Damn! He'd been traveling a lot and competing hard, and he hadn't had much time for a social life.

He needed a woman.

Badly.

Knowing that woman couldn't be Mary Beth, he approached her with trepidation, wanting to touch her, but knowing he needed to rein in his awareness of her.

"Mary Beth," he called, lowering his voice so he wouldn't startle her.

She didn't move.

Okay, so now you're going to have to touch her.

His palms felt sweaty, and he rubbed them on his jeans.

You wanted an excuse to, anyway.

Yeah, he did. Crouching beside her, he called to her again as he gently shook her shoulder. "Come on, sweetheart. Wake up."

She came awake slowly, then focused her green eyes on him. She sat up and sucked in a quick breath.

"Deke! What are you doing here?" She hadn't expected him to be there, and just thinking about him hanging around while she'd been sleeping was unnerving.

Deke didn't move. "I stayed for a while to be sure you were okay."

Figuring she must look a sight, Mary Beth raised a hand to her hair, then brushed several strands of it from her face.

"You didn't need to. As you can see, I'm perfectly fine." She tugged on her shirt and straightened it.

"Yeah, you keep saying that." His gaze skimmed her face. "Here," he said, assisting her as she started to stand. "I'll help you to the kitchen. I made some dinner for you."

She stilled. "You what?"

He chuckled at her stunned expression. "Don't get too excited. You haven't tasted it yet." An easy grin formed on his lips.

"I can walk," she insisted, not wanting him to touch her. She tried to push his hands away as she struggled to her feet.

Deke sighed with frustration. Her ankle was still quite swollen, and he knew it had to hurt. "Humor me, huh?" Sliding his arm around her shoulders, he held one of her hands as she half walked, half limped to the kitchen.

Mary Beth eased onto a chair at the table. "What's that I smell?"

"Damn!" Deke made a beeline for the oven, jerked open the door and, using a battered pot holder, removed the tray of overbrowned biscuits. Disappointment outlined his features. "I think they're a little overdone," he stated, frowning as he put them on a plate and placed them on the table.

Her stomach growling, Mary Beth reached for one. Steam rose from the biscuit as she pulled it apart and took a bite. "They're not too bad," she assured him in an effort to make him feel better. "You didn't have to do all this, Deke."

He shrugged and joined her at the table, easing onto the chair next to her. It wasn't a big deal, and he didn't want her to read anything into it. "I was getting hungry, and I thought you'd be hungry, too."

She smiled at him, her appreciation genuine. "I am hungry, and this looks delicious."

Deke stopped in the middle of biting his biscuit. It was the first time Mary Beth had smiled since he'd arrived, and he felt the force of it all the way to his toes. Her hair, mussed from sleeping, made him want to run his hands through it, which made him want to kiss her, which made him want to...

"Is something wrong?" Mary Beth asked, watching him. He was staring at her as if she'd lost her front tooth.

Deke blinked. "What? No, sorry, I was, um, thinking about something," he finished lamely, and he told himself to get a grip on his libido.

Mary Beth looked as confused as he felt, but thankfully, she let it drop as she slid some noodles and sauce onto her fork. Deke tried to look anywhere but at her. He saw the stack of old magazines he'd pushed aside earlier to make room on the table, and it reminded him of the picture on the refrigerator.

"Are you planning a trip?" he asked, attacking his food.

Startled by his question, Mary Beth stared at him. "No, why?"

He nodded at the stack of magazines on the table. "All of these travel magazines and that picture of Mexico on your fridge." Pointing to it with his fork, he continued, "I thought maybe you were planning a trip."

Her cheeks reddened, and she shook her head. "No, I'm not going anywhere."

"Did you have to cancel a trip when you came home?"

She finished chewing a bite of the noodles. "No." It was probably ridiculous for her to have hauled the magazines back here when she'd returned. But all of her life she'd wanted out of Crockett. Every day she caught herself dreaming of other cities, other countries, living anywhere but here.

But she wasn't ready to admit to Deke or anyone else that she was trying to make the ranch a success so she could leave. Considering the shape it was in, he'd think that was downright laughable. Out of the corner of her eye she could see he was waiting for her to explain. Oh, God, how could she? She was foolish to believe that she'd one day live someplace exotic when she didn't even have enough money to make minor repairs on the ranch.

Clearing her throat, she put down her fork. "I just like looking through them. After working so hard on the ranch every day, reading the stories and looking at the pictures helps me relax."

He frowned thoughtfully as he digested her explanation. "Really?" Deke wasn't quite sure why, but he had the suspicion there was more to it than that. A telling factor was the glowing red color on her cheeks and neck. He suppressed the urge to press her. "I'll have to try that sometime."

Mary Beth glanced his way, and he winked. Her chest constricted. He was making fun of her. "You think that's funny?"

Sobering, Deke shook his head. "Absolutely not. I've never been to Mexico, but I can see the appeal of lying on a beach like that." He nodded his head at the picture, drawing her attention to it. The thought of lying naked with Mary Beth on a deserted beach did crazy things to his self-control.

Her gaze slid over to the picture and landed on the lovers. She got his meaning. "Yes, well—" She cleared her throat. "I kept the picture for the scenery," she quickly asserted, her eyes coming back to meet his. She tried her best not to imagine lying on a deserted beach with Deke, his hard naked body on hers, but her mind displayed the image with graphic clarity. Geez, it suddenly felt hot in the room. Mary Beth nearly groaned. It was an effort not to fan herself.

"Ah." He drained the tea from his glass and shoved his chair back. "How about it, sweetheart? Wanna run off to Mexico together?" He knew he shouldn't tease her, but he couldn't help himself. He liked watching her blush.

Gathering a modicum of self-control, Mary Beth feigned a shocked expression. "And deprive all those buckle bunnies around the rodeo of your company? I wouldn't think of it," she answered, intentionally widening her eyes. "I've heard tell that if you're a big bad bull rider, you can have your pick of women."

Deke opened his mouth to deny the charge, but had to catch himself. There *were* plenty of women who hung around the rodeo, and admittedly he hadn't turned a blind eye to them. But those women knew the score. They were nothing like Mary Beth. They were looking for a good time, not for happily-ever-after.

"Don't believe everything you hear," he said, deciding to play that part of rodeo life down. He wasn't about to give her a reason to lower her opinion of him even more. "If you're finished," he said, abruptly getting to his feet, "I'll clean this up."

"You don't need to," Mary Beth rushed to tell him. "I'll take care of them later."

"Don't worry about it. It won't take me that long."

"Deke—"

He scowled down at her. "Do you have to fight me on everything?"

"Do you have to be so obstinate about everything?" she countered.

Deke mentally began counting to ten. He got to five and

felt more in control. "Look, why don't you go in and watch television or something? I'll take care of this mess, then get out of your hair." At her disbelieving expression, he drew an invisible cross over his heart. "I promise."

Giving up, Mary Beth sighed heavily. "I think I'll just get ready for bed." When she started to get up, Deke grasped her arm. To prove she could walk on her own, she put a little weight on her ankle. The sudden jolt of pain made her wince. "Oh!"

Deke swore under his breath as he swept her up in his arms again. "Hold on." His gut clenched when she slid her arms around his neck. "Don't say a word, woman," he cautioned, his eyes dark and stormy.

Mary Beth clamped her lips together as he carried her through the house to her bedroom. Once there, he deposited her gently on her bed, then looked around the small room. Satisfied she could reach her dresser from the bed, he turned his gaze back on her.

"I'll leave you to get ready." He pointed a finger at her. "Don't get off that bed. When you're ready, call out, and I'll help you to the bathroom."

"Yes, sir." She gave him a military salute.

"Someday that smart mouth and sassy attitude's gonna get you into trouble."

"I'm scared." It was obvious she wasn't.

Deke's gaze ran intimately over her. "You should be."

Mary Beth watched him storm from the room. What on earth was wrong with her? All she had to do was bide her time, thank Deke for everything and watch him walk out of her life the way he'd done so easily two years ago. But no. She couldn't do that. Instead, she'd gone out of her way to provoke him.

It just wasn't in her nature to let another man run roughshod over her. She'd had enough of that from her father.

She no longer had to listen to anyone tell her what she could or couldn't do.

"Especially Deke," she muttered, scooting to the edge of the bed. Pushing off, she hopped on one foot to the closet, opened the door, then took her nightgown and robe off of a hook.

Knowing he'd probably return at any moment, she struggled out of her clothes and tossed them on a nearby chair. Quickly she slipped on her nightgown and robe. Instead of waiting like Deke told her, she opened the door. Limping and hopping, she made her way to the bathroom in the hall.

She looked longingly at the tub, then decided there was no way she was going to get naked and take a bath with Deke McCall in her house. Then she caught a look at herself in the mirror and gasped. A wild mass of her curls had escaped her barrette and fell around her face in disarray. She removed the barrette, brushed the tangles out, then subdued it behind her neck again.

It took her a few more minutes to wash her face and brush her teeth. When she was ready to leave, she unlocked the door and opened it. Silently she peeked out into the hallway. Deke wasn't anywhere in sight. Breathing a sigh of relief, she started to make her way back to her room with the same techniques she'd used to get to the bathroom. About halfway back to her room, she tripped when her foot caught on a throw rug. Trying to catch herself, she put all of her weight on her injured ankle.

She couldn't help screaming as the floor came up to meet her. Before she could get her bearings, the sound of Deke's boots pounding on the hardwood floor told her he'd heard her fall.

"Dammit, Mary Beth, I told you to wait!" His eyes narrowed as he stared at her sprawled on the floor, and his fingers tightened on the compress in his hand. Kneeling beside her, he lifted her and once again carried her to her bedroom. "You have got to be the most stubborn woman I've ever met!"

"I was trying to—"

"I know," Deke said, gritting his teeth. Didn't she realize she was doing more harm to herself? "You wanted to do it yourself." Lowering her to the bed, he sat beside her and held on to her when she tried to scoot away. "Are you all right?" he asked, running his gaze over her, the irritation in his voice nearly gone.

"Yes. I'm fine." Mary Beth's response came out a whisper as she became aware of their intimate surroundings, of how good it felt to be touched by him. She stared at his blond hair as he ran his big hands over her arms, checking for bruises. He was sitting so close that she could see each single strand, so close that it would only take a slight move on her part to be in his arms.

Seeing that she looked as if she hadn't done any damage to herself, Deke lifted his face to hers, and their eyes locked. He lost all sense of thought as his hands gripped her shoulders. Her scent surrounded him, stealing his ability to do something as simple as breathe.

He should let her go. It would be the smart thing to do. But Deke wasn't thinking about being smart. All he could think about is what it would feel like to kiss her again.

"Look, I'm really sorry for yelling at you," he said, his voice suddenly hoarse.

"It's all right." As if mesmerized, her eyes stayed on his.

"No, it isn't. You're going through a rough time. I should have been more patient." His gaze dropped to her mouth. Her lips were perfectly sculpted, ripe for kissing.

For his kisses. His gut tightened another notch.

"You don't have to be superwoman, Mary Beth. It isn't a crime to let others help you." Tears crested her eyes, and he realized then just how important it was for her to make the running of the ranch a success.

"I...I can't..." She stopped speaking and turned her head aside, unable to get the words out without weeping. She *wasn't* going to humiliate herself further in front of Deke.

Deke couldn't stand the defeat he saw in her expression. But it was there, along with the despair in her eyes. He cupped her face, forcing her to look at him. "Hang in there, Red," he whispered, brushing his knuckles across her cheek in a soft caress. "Everything will work out."

Calling her by her nickname provoked his desired effect. Her eyes chilled considerably.

"Don't—"

"Call you Red," he finished for her. An understanding smile tugged at his lips. "Yeah, I know." He searched her expression, relieved to see that the anxiety in her eyes had eased.

She gave him a fragile smile. "Thanks."

"You're welcome." He didn't smile back. His senses reeled, and her warmth lured him closer. "Mary Beth," he murmured, when her tongue slipped out and moistened her lips. He cupped the back of her head, tilting her face up to his.

Her lips parted, and their breaths mingled. Deke's mouth slowly closed over hers, gently, briefly, then again with more pressure. Fire exploded throughout his body. Her palm came up against his chest, and it was all he could do not to crawl into the bed with her and strip her naked.

He sure wanted to.

He deepened the kiss, sliding his tongue into her mouth, touching the tip of hers. She moaned, a deep, longing sound that was enough to break the spell between them. He pulled away from her and got abruptly to his feet. Tasting her on his lips, he swore softly to himself.

What had he almost done?

This damn habit of comforting Mary Beth was getting totally out of control. He opened his mouth to speak, to apologize, but nothing came out. Then he did the unthinkable for the second time in his life.

He got the hell out of there.

Four

You should have stayed away. You're only going to hurt her again.

Squinting from the early-morning sun, Deke traveled the road between the Bar M and Paradise, his foot momentarily hesitating over the brake pedal. He ignored the warning of his conscience, shifted his boot and mashed down on the gas. This was the right thing to do, he told himself. He was only going to check on Mary Beth.

Because you can't stay away.

No, that wasn't true, he argued with himself. She didn't have anyone helping her. It was the least he could do. And he needed to apologize to her. He owed her that much.

Yet even now, thoughts of holding her in his arms again made him want a whole lot more.

Okay, you're not even going to think about the kiss.

Just apologize. Straight-out. Sincere, but to the point.

The memory of that kiss continued to haunt him. It had

been a mistake in more ways than one. First off, he'd enjoyed it too much. Secondly, he hadn't wanted to stop at a kiss. It had taken every single ounce of his strength to pull away from her. Mary Beth was a pleasure that wasn't his to have.

Kissing her had been a conscious choice. In the back of his mind, he'd thought to prove to himself that she was a temptation he could resist.

He'd been wrong.

Maybe he'd resisted her last night, but that one kiss had taught him that he still wanted her. What was he going to do about it? If he had any sense of self-preservation, he'd turn his truck around and head out of town.

Instead he braked, slowing down his truck to a speed just this side of dangerous for the curve ahead, then took the turn leading to Paradise. His truck bounced in and out of every hole in the dusty road before he pulled to a stop in front of her small ranch house.

Letting the engine idle, he absently stared out the front window of his truck and tried to dig up the nerve to go in and apologize for his disappearing act the night before. Without thinking twice about it, he could climb on the back of a thousand-pound bull full of power and rage. Why did facing Mary Beth seem like a fate worse than death?

Because you hurt her.

Again.

A tightness in his gut confirmed his thoughts. The wounded look in her eyes had haunted him all night. Running on just a couple of hours of sleep, he felt anxious and irritable. All because of what he'd done to her.

Well, hell, at least he was doing the right thing now.

Determined to get his apology over with before he chickened out, Deke grabbed his hat from the seat and slapped it on his head as he exited the truck. A movement at the side of the house caught his eye. Spotting Mary Beth, he came to an abrupt halt. Limping, she struggled to keep her balance as she walked.

''Mary Beth!'' Her head swung in his direction, then just as quickly away. Deke crossed the yard, his heels kicking up dust. He glanced at the sunny, blue sky. The storm that had threatened last night had never arrived. But from Mary Beth's cold expression, he had a feeling he was about to face a storm of a different kind—a fury he well deserved.

Mary Beth's steps faltered, then she recovered and disappeared around the corner of the house.

Deke! Oh, God! What was he doing here? And dammit, why did her heart do a special little beat at the sight of him?

She clenched her fists. How dare he show up this morning? After the way he'd treated her last night, he could go to hell. She'd thought he'd changed. He'd made this big pretense of wanting to help her, wanting to make sure she was all right. Foolishly she'd let down her guard.

Then he'd kissed her.

She'd safeguarded her heart for two years, and with a single kiss Deke had chiseled away at that solid wall she'd built around it. Little cracks had appeared, revealing her vulnerability to him. But she wasn't going to let him hurt her again. While she had no plans to become involved with him, she was smart enough to know that her heart was still in danger. She'd had feelings for him most of her life. Now she just had to keep from letting herself get further involved with him.

Carefully, she managed the back steps as quickly as she could and went inside, knowing that Deke would be right behind her. She grabbed a glass from the cabinet, then opened the refrigerator and took out a pitcher of cold water.

Then she heard the back door open.

"What the hell are you doing walking on your ankle?" Deke demanded, stepping into the room. He whipped off his hat and tossed it on the kitchen table. At the sound of his voice, Mary Beth's shoulders visibly tightened. Busy pouring water into a glass, she didn't even acknowledge that she'd heard him come into the room. But her stiffened spine gave her awareness of him away.

"Mary Beth—"

Mary Beth slammed the pitcher down on the counter with a thud. She whirled around to face him, crossing her arms over her chest. "Don't you dare yell at me!"

"I wouldn't, if you didn't give me reason to," Deke retorted.

"You're accusing me—"

"No," he said, lowering his voice. "I didn't mean to make it sound like that." His lips thinned as he glanced at her foot. "You need to get off your ankle." He nodded his head toward a kitchen chair.

Mary Beth didn't move. "What are you doing here, Deke?"

He winced from the ice in her tone. "I wanted to talk to you."

Her hand went to her hip. "So, go ahead and talk. I'm not stopping you." But she didn't continue looking at him. Instead, she turned her back on him and grasped the glass with both hands.

Deke sucked in a hard breath. He wanted to see her face, wanted to gauge the reaction in her eyes. "Could you just look at me?"

"You don't owe me any explanations," Mary Beth said coolly.

"Yes, I do." Still, she ignored him. He wasn't going to apologize to her back. "Look at me," he demanded, his tone rougher than he intended.

Remaining silent, she lifted the glass and drank. Deke swore under his breath. He wanted to get his apology over with, to clear his conscience so he could think about something other than her.

You need to get your mind on the next competition.

The tight standings between Deke and two other cowboys was enough pressure without throwing his awareness of Mary Beth into the fray. He couldn't afford to get distracted. This year he had a real chance of taking the title in Las Vegas, but only if he could keep his mind on bull riding and off his sexy neighbor.

"Mary Beth," he implored, softening his voice. She set the glass on the counter but still didn't move. Deke cursed again. The woman had a way of testing his patience. "Please."

As he reached out to touch her shoulder, she swung around to face him, anger and humiliation taut in her expression. Amidst those emotions, there was also pain. He let his hand drop. He'd done that, he thought, guilt eating at his heart. He'd caused that fragile hurt in her eyes. Now and two years ago. Back then he hadn't waited around to explain. Her haunted expression caused his chest to tighten.

"I just…I want to talk to you."

"All right," she told him, her stance wary. "You have my undivided attention."

She wasn't going to make it easy for him. Well, that was okay. She had a right to be angry. There was nothing she could say or do that would make him feel worse than he already did. Nothing. Because he felt as low as any man could. Why did he seem to hurt the people he cared about the most?

"I'm sorry, Mary Beth," he said. "I shouldn't have run out on you like that."

Mary Beth didn't even blink. "Which time, Deke? Last night or two years ago?" Her chin came up a notch. Her retort had wounded him. She'd seen the flash of regret in his eyes. So why didn't she feel as if she'd scored a point, or at least regained a fraction of her pride?

"Last night," he clarified solemnly. He didn't want to talk about two years ago. That was over. History. To apologize for what happened between them two years ago would require him to lie to her, and he couldn't bring himself to do that. "It isn't you, I swear. It's me."

"Well, thank you, Deke. That makes me feel so much better." She feigned a bright smile. "Now that you've gotten that off your chest, you can leave."

Annoyed that she'd so easily dismissed him, Deke shrugged his shoulders as he looked around. "I thought maybe I could lend you a hand. You shouldn't be walking on that ankle yet."

"No, thanks." She gave him a disinterested look, then started to turn away.

He caught her shoulder with his hand and drew her to a halt. Despite an inner warning that told him he was treading on dangerous territory, Deke forged ahead with his plan to help her. "I could keep an eye on things around here, help take care of you." Her eyes narrowed. "Just for today," he clarified.

Mary Beth's curiosity got the best of her. "Aren't you returning to the rodeo?" She prayed that he was. The last thing she needed was Deke hanging around, having him so near would be disastrous to her heart. She could resist him—at least she really believed she could—if he wasn't underfoot all the time.

"I'll be returning to competition tomorrow, yeah. Until then, I can help out around here."

"I don't want your help."

The lie rolled off her tongue easily. The idea of someone watching over her was more appealing than she wanted to admit—even to herself. She'd never had the luxury of having someone care about her, think about or anticipate her needs. She'd always been the caregiver. The thought of Deke watching out for her was frighteningly alluring.

Deke frowned. He should've known that she'd be stubborn about it. Heck, last night she'd almost broken her leg hopping back to bed instead of waiting for him to help her. "Whether you like it or not, you *need* help."

She shrugged his hand from her arm while she still had the ability to carry off an iota of bravado. "I don't want to depend on anyone, and that *especially* includes *you.*" The ranch was probably going under, anyway. She might be able to delay it for a while, but the end result seemed inevitable.

Deke's jaw hardened. "Accepting help never seemed to bother your father."

Mary Beth drew in a sharp breath. How dare he compare her to her father! It was true that Hank Adams had always been quick to call on neighboring ranchers for help, but she was nothing like him.

Nothing. And she resented the implication.

"Leave my father out of this," she warned him. More disturbing was the fact that Deke had the power to hurt her. She had to say something, *anything,* to get rid of him, to get him out of her life. He was a complication she didn't need. "Having your help for a day won't make a bit of difference around here," she insisted. "I'll be on my own after you're gone."

"It *will* make a difference," he pressed, already regretting the crack he'd made about her father. He was trying to gain ground with her and instead he was losing it. "It'll give your ankle a chance to heal. Maybe I can help you find someone to take over for Clyde."

Mary Beth could hardly admit that she didn't have the money to hire someone to replace her ranch hand. "My ankle's not that bad. I can do my own chores."

"Let me see it," Deke stated.

"What?" she asked, her eyes widening.

"Let me see your ankle." He didn't wait for her to agree. Giving her a choice would only cause more aggravation between them, and Lord knew they'd had enough of that already. Bending down, he lifted her foot and pulled her boot off before she had a chance to protest. Then he shoved her sock down, revealing the bandage she'd wrapped around her ankle. In seconds he'd unwrapped it. "Dammit, Mary Beth, it's still swollen!"

"It's better than it was yesterday."

"Maybe so, but it'll heal quicker if you take it easy another day. Go into the living room and get off it." He gave her a stern look when she didn't move. "Right now. I'll get you some ice."

She opened her mouth to challenge him, but his next words stopped her.

"Do it, or I'll cart you in there myself."

Her expression indignant, Mary Beth clamped her lips together. Without another word, she snatched her boot from him and limped from the room with as much dignity as she could muster.

Deke watched her disappear though the doorway. She had an obstinate side to her, that was for sure, he thought, as he prepared an ice pack. Why did he find that side of her just as appealing? Shaking his head, he went into the living room. She was sitting on the couch, her foot elevated. She didn't speak as he approached her, but he felt the cold chill of her gaze.

"Keep off it," he ordered, undaunted. He settled an ice pack on her ankle. "I'm going out for a while. I'll be back to check on you."

Deke didn't wait for her to answer. Rather than tempting fate by staying with her, he went outside to pick up where she'd left off. As he entered the barn, he saw that she hadn't even started feeding the horses, so he figured she couldn't have been on her ankle all that long.

He located the hay—at least, what there was of it. There was only half a bale. Wondering if she had the rest of it stored in one of the other buildings, he made a mental note to ask her about it.

Hours later Deke stepped into Mary Beth's house, unsure of the reception he'd receive from his unwilling patient. He hadn't meant to intimidate her or to make her angry, but the woman didn't seem to know what was good for her.

He'd spent the better part of the morning tending to the horses, then riding out and checking her cattle. It was a good thing that he had. He'd found another break in her fencing. By the time he'd gotten the tools and had it repaired, he'd realized that he was getting hungry. While he should have gotten in his truck and headed back to the Bar M, Deke wanted to check on Mary Beth.

When he walked inside, she was sitting on the sofa in the living room, her foot propped up on a beat-up ottoman. His heart rate accelerated. At least she'd listened to him.

"How's it feel?" he asked. He sat on the sofa, careful

to keep his distance from her. Removing his hat, he set it aside, then combed his hair with his fingers.

"Better," she said, her voice tight.

"That's good." Deke doubted it. He itched to check it, but knew if he did, he'd just make her angrier. But then, maybe that was a good idea. Maybe if she was angry with him, he wouldn't be so tempted to kiss her.

Risking her ire, he lifted the ice pack and examined her ankle. He was surprised and pleased to see that her injury did look better. Minimally, but there was a sign of improvement. It was still slightly swollen and several shades of purple. "Yeah," he agreed. "It looks like it's healing." Maybe by tomorrow it would be hurt less and she'd be able to walk on it again without making it worse.

He sure hoped so. He didn't like the idea of leaving her on her own, unable to get around.

"I made you some lunch," she informed him, a bit of resentment in her tone. "Don't worry," she said before he could speak, "I was careful. I put everything on the table and sat down to do it. There's also some soup warming on the stove. It's canned, but it was all I had." When she'd gone to the bathroom, she'd peeked out the window and had seen that his truck was still in front of her house. She hadn't expected him to stay that long, but since he had, she figured he'd be hungry when he came in.

A pleasurable sensation tingled up Deke's spine. While he wanted to admonish her for being up and around, he couldn't bring himself to do so. Making him lunch had been the first nice thing she'd done for him since he'd walked back into her life. It also told him that she'd been checking on his whereabouts. That deepened the feeling of pleasure, and Deke knew he'd have to be very careful to keep his sentiments for Mary Beth under control. "I'm starving, that's for sure," he said, grinning at her. "What about you? Have you eaten yet?"

She shook her head. "I'm not really hungry."

"Come and keep me company while I eat, then." He stood and held out his hand to her.

Mary Beth's first reaction was to rebuke his offer of help. But she tamped down that instinct, thinking if she went along with him, she'd be better off. He'd be leaving soon enough. Knowing that, she wouldn't be foolish enough to put any real trust in him. And during the time he was here, he *could* get a lot more done around the ranch than she would be able to do on a bad ankle.

Putting her hand in his, she relied on his strength to help her off the couch. His scent surrounded her, and she quickly let go of his hand and put some space between them so she wouldn't give in to her desire to lean against him. She was pleased when Deke kept quiet as she used her own fortitude to get to the kitchen. In any case, he was close by her side until she took a seat at the table.

"The sandwiches are in the refrigerator," she told him, pointing to it.

Deke nodded. He retrieved them, then set the plate on the table and unwrapped the cellophane covering it. Though each sandwich wasn't loaded with lunch meat, there were a lot of them. Once again, he wondered about her financial status.

It took him a few minutes to get some ice in the glasses and pour the tea she'd prepared, then he moved the pot of vegetable soup to the table. Though Mary Beth had said that she wasn't hungry, he got an extra bowl and plate from the cabinet, hoping that she'd join him.

He didn't say anything to her, just put the setting before her along with her drink. "I found another break in your fencing," he mentioned as he took a seat at the table. "It just needed a little repair before it got worse. The cattle are okay, but if it's all right with you, I thought I'd move them to another pasture tomorrow. It looks like they've about done as much grazing as they can where they are.''

"That'll be fine.'' She'd been planning to do that, as well—that is, along with Clyde's help.

"Why don't you join me?'' he suggested, indicating the soup and sandwiches. "You might not be hungry, but you need to eat. And to tell you the truth, I don't like eating alone. I do enough of that on the road. It's kinda nice to share a meal with someone other than the guys on the rodeo.''

Did that mean that he didn't *always* have a woman with him? Her heart leaped at the thought as she looked at the food. The smell of the warm soup *had* stirred her hunger. And maybe she could eat one sandwich. "Okay.'' She wondered about his comment.

Don't be a fool, her mind taunted.

Her lips turned slightly upward as Deke ladled some soup into a bowl for her. She reached for a sandwich. "You should be home spending time with your family. I feel bad keeping you from them.''

He chuckled. "You're not keeping me from them. Everyone at the ranch is busy working. They don't stop to entertain me when I come home for a few days.''

"I saw Matt in town last week,'' Mary Beth mentioned. "He sure has grown since he came to live at the Bar M.'' She'd first met Deke's nephew over a year ago. Nearly thirteen, he'd come to Crockett in search of the father he never knew. He'd been hitchhiking and she'd given him a ride when he'd asked where the McCalls lived. She hadn't known then that Catherine, Matt's mother, had been Jake's college sweetheart, whom he'd left when he'd had to come home and raise his siblings when his parents had been killed.

It was obvious to everyone who met him that Matt was Jake's son. Tall and muscled from working on the ranch, he had his father's height and build.

"Yeah," Deke agreed. He lifted his glass and took a long drink of the tea. "He's going on fifteen now and already looking forward to driving. Catherine is the principal at the high school."

"I'd heard that." She ate a spoonful of the soup, then said, "I haven't talked to Ashley in a while. How are the kids?"

His eyes softened. "The twins are into nearly everything. She has her hands full keeping up with them and their little brother, Taylor. But Ashley's doing a fantastic job of mothering them."

After saving Ashley from the advances of a drunken cowboy, Ryder had spent the night with her. Though he hadn't meant to steal her virtue, when he later found out she was pregnant, he'd convinced her to live at the Bar M until the baby was born. They'd ended up falling in love, getting married and having twins.

Ashley living with them had been one of the best things that had ever happened to the family, especially Deke. He'd loved having a woman around the house, and Ashley had doted on him.

Mary Beth was very aware that Deke's entire demeanor had changed when he spoke of his sister-in-law. Stunned by sudden feelings of jealousy, she tried to think of something to say to steer the subject in another direction. "Um, I got a chance to meet Catherine's sister at Jake and Catherine's wedding. She seemed really nice."

She didn't know why she'd even brought up Bethany St. John. Sitting back in her chair, Mary Beth admonished herself. She'd brought up another woman who was actually *available* to him!

Well, she didn't *really* care. She had no reason to feel even remotely possessive of Deke.

Deke smiled as he reached for his third sandwich. "She left for Virginia right after the wedding. As a matter of fact, I took her to the airport on my way to San Antonio. She's really sweet, a lot like Catherine," he went on, and his eyes twinkled.

"I only talked with her a few minutes," she admitted. In her mind she pictured Deke with Bethany. Sweet, he'd said. And beautiful, Mary Beth thought to herself, her lips tightening. She wished that she'd never brought the woman up. Bethany St. John looked like Catherine, with thick chocolate-brown hair and a voluptuous figure. Even though he spoke casually about her, surely Deke had noticed. Any normal man within a few feet of her would have.

He finished the last bite of his sandwich. "She's planning to visit in the spring. I'll make sure you get a chance to get acquainted." He finished his glass of tea. "Oh," he said, changing the subject, "I used what was left of the hay. If you tell me where the rest is stored, I'll move it into the barn."

Mary Beth sat up straight, then fiddled with her spoon. "I knew it was getting low."

Deke looked at her. "You don't have any more?"

She shook her head, and a heavy sigh escaped her lips. "I was going to pick some up a couple of days ago." Her gaze dropped to the table.

"You're not growing it?" Deke asked, curious. It wasn't like Mary Beth to not plan ahead. Or was it? He was discovering there was a lot about her he didn't know.

A lump formed in her throat. She managed to swallow

past it, but her teeth worried her lower lip. "I haven't had much success. I've been buying it in town. At least I was until my truck broke down. I tried to figure out what was wrong with it, but never could get the darn thing started. Clyde was going to take a look at it." She shrugged one shoulder. "Now, he's quit. I guess in all the confusion, I forgot to get the hay." She'd have to call the feed store and have it brought out, which would cost money she didn't have to spare.

Deke stood and took his dishes to the sink. "I'm no ace mechanic, but I'll take a look at your truck. If I can't figure out what's wrong, Russ can come over and check it out." Russ was married to his sister, Lynn, and they owned a horse ranch about ten minutes away. "He's had a lot of odd jobs over the years. I bet he can fix it." He returned to the table to pick up her dishes, then took them to the sink, Mary Beth's financial situation on his mind.

Had she really forgotten to order the feed? It didn't seem to him that she had that much money, but he wasn't sure. Hell, if she was short of cash, he'd lend her some. He opened his mouth to make the offer, then shut it again. Maybe he'd better wait for further proof before jumping to conclusions. Besides, they were actually getting along for the moment. And he was beginning to enjoy it.

"Please don't go to any trouble," she insisted. Mary Beth didn't want Deke to involve anyone else in her problems.

Deke walked back over to the table and stopped beside her. "Don't worry about it." He lifted her face up so he could look into her eyes. "Stop frowning or you're gonna have worry lines," he warned, then drew his finger across her forehead. He'd only meant to tease, but the instant his fingers touched her face, his body tightened and the last of his words spilled out in a rough ache.

Mary Beth's breath dammed in her lungs as she stared at him. She hadn't expected him to touch her. An intense sensation of longing flared deep in her stomach.

You've really got to get a grip on your attraction to this man.

She swallowed hard and tried to smile. "I'll remember that."

Desire stirred inside Deke. Lustful feelings that he had no business entertaining. The last thing he needed was to get involved with Mary Beth. But as sure as he was that it was going to complicate things between them, he had a suspicion that getting involved with her was something he wasn't going to be able to stop.

Five

Deke pushed Mary Beth's pickup truck under the shade of an old pecan tree. Though the vehicle wasn't a relic, it sure hadn't seen a showroom in years. Rust had eaten away at the dull silver paint along the front fender and left ugly jagged holes in its wake.

Even if he got it started, he didn't like the idea of Mary Beth traveling the roads in this beat-up, unsafe truck. It could break down miles from town on one of the back roads. Stuck out in the middle of nowhere, anything could happen to her.

As he worked on the truck, checking plugs and cleaning off connections, Mary Beth's situation nagged at him, darkening his mood. The hay for the horses was gone and her pantry was practically bare. On top of that, the ranch all but screamed for attention. Either she didn't care about the desperate need of repairs, or she had much greater problems. He suspected the latter.

If she had any sense, she'd sell the ranch. It was a good piece of land with the potential to be profitable. Why was she holding on to it? Stubborn woman. Yeah, if he'd learned nothing else about her, he'd definitely learned she was stubborn.

And sexy as hell.

Oh, yeah. All he could think about was making love to her. All night long. He had erotic memories of the night he'd spent with her. Every single detail was etched in his brain. Being around her today had made him cognizant of his physical awareness of her. How could he not want to make love to her now?

Well, so what if he did? he argued with himself. It didn't mean he had a thing for her.

"Ow!" He jerked his finger back as it connected with a live wire. He'd better keep his mind on the engine before he fried his brain. Not that Mary Beth wasn't doing a fine job of that as it was.

It wasn't long after he checked the headlights and ensured they worked fine that he ruled out the battery. Although old, it appeared to be sufficiently charged. However, come winter, it'd probably have to be replaced.

Scratching his cheek, he couldn't imagine sinking any more money into the old heap. Apparently, maintaining the truck wasn't high on Mary Beth's list of priorities. Pulling out the oil dip stick, he shook his head. A black, gooey syrup that he presumed to be oil clung to it. Not to mention it was a quart low. He shook his head and wondered when she'd last had it changed.

More proof that Mary Beth needed money?

And what else hadn't she mentioned? Maybe she'd been short and couldn't pay Clyde. Was that why he'd quit? If so, it meant that she wouldn't be able to afford to hire someone to take his place.

He pondered that thought as he continued checking parts on the truck. He figured he'd test his theory of her money troubles later, mention she should buy a newer model truck, then gauge her response.

In the end the problem with her truck turned out to be the alternator. Deke made a trip into town to pick up a new one, then decided to swing by the feed store for hay and feed. More than likely Mary Beth wouldn't like it, but if she was really in financial straits, he'd be saving her the delivery charge.

Besides, he couldn't stand the thought that if she got it in her head to pick up the supplies, she'd try to unload the bales by herself. Deke more than anyone else knew that once she got something on her mind, it took a stick of dynamite to make her change it.

Upon returning, Deke moved the hay and feed to the barn, then installed the new alternator, racing against what looked like another storm moving in. As he scanned the darkening sky, he could smell the cool scent of the incoming rain, feel the potency of the storm in the air. He glanced at the parched ground. They could use it.

Years ago at the Bar M, he and his brothers had installed an elaborate irrigation system. Not all ranchers had the resources to do the same. Deke shook his head in disgust as he looked over Mary Beth's dry, cracked land. It was a shame that Hank hadn't seen fit to invest the time and expense on irrigation for Paradise. If the right care were given, this ranch could be one of the finest around. One even he would be proud to own.

He turned his attention back to the truck and tightened the last bolt one more time. Sweat dripped from his forehead, and he wiped it from his brow with the bottom of his dirty, dark-blue T-shirt. Hoping that he'd solved the problem, he got inside the truck and gave the key a twist.

The engine turned over, sputtered, then began running more smoothly. He switched it off, then tried it again, and it started right up.

Distant thunder rumbled as he started toward the house to check on Mary Beth. He frowned at the churning clouds as drops of water dotted his shirt. Just as he reached the door and stepped inside, the sky let loose.

He'd deliberately stayed outside all afternoon, determined to prove to himself that he could resist the temptation of being with her. A waste of time, he thought now as he hurried through the kitchen, calling her name. As much as he'd told himself that he could keep his distance, he was anxious to let her know that he'd fixed her truck. Oddly, doing something for her, however small, gave him a sense of satisfaction.

Unaware that she'd been sleeping, he walked into the living room. As he hung his hat on a rack, she jumped and stared at him, her eyes wide and soft.

"Sorry. I didn't mean to wake you."

She stretched her arms above her head, her body moving provocatively in slow motion, lifting her full breasts, jutting them at him. Deke thought for sure that he was being tested. He stared at her with his tongue practically hanging out. Hell, he was only human.

"It's okay." Mary Beth sleepily rubbed her eyes, then opened them again. She scooted into a sitting position.

It was far from okay from where he was standing, Deke thought. "How's your ankle?"

"I think it's getting better. It doesn't hurt nearly as much now." She removed the ice pack so he could see, then winced as she ran her hand over the injury.

"That's good." He bent down to inspect it. Actually, she was right. It did look better. The swelling was down and the bruising had faded a little.

"What time is it?" she asked, looking up at him as he examined her ankle.

"Almost six." His gaze traveled up the length of her leg, slowly over her body and stopped at her face. Just looking at her made him want to touch her.

She frowned at his shirt, smeared with black smudges of grease, then at his greasy hands. "You've been working on my truck all this time?"

"Not exactly. I needed a part for it, so I ran into town. I finished just as it started to rain." He decided not to mention that he'd picked up the supplies she'd needed. That bit of information could wait. Right now she wasn't mad at him. Not knowing how long *that* would last, Deke wanted to just enjoy being with her.

Fat drops began pelting the roof. Mary Beth jumped at a sharp clap of thunder. "Which part?"

Deke watched her comb her hair into place with her hands. "The alternator. Your truck's running now, but you really should replace the battery before the weather turns cold. And it wouldn't hurt to get an oil change, either."

Mary Beth's face grew hot. She'd meant to take care of the maintenance on the truck, but she hadn't wanted to spare the money. Not yet. Not until she'd paid her mortgage. "I know it's overdue. I haven't had time to get to it."

Deke straightened and stepped away from her, afraid he'd do something totally stupid like reach for her. Leaning his shoulder against the wall, he said casually, "Don't put it off too long. And I added a quart of oil. That'll hold you for a while. Better yet, why don't you replace that death trap?"

Mary Beth stiffened. She just couldn't admit she was holding on to the ranch by a thread. "I like that old truck," she lied, hoping he wouldn't see through her deception. "I'm not ready to get rid of it."

Deke studied her expression, noticed the red splotches on her cheeks and neck. He didn't believe her for a minute, but he let it go. "It's your decision," he said with a shrug.

She nodded, then swung her feet to the floor. "I appreciate your working on it, though. How much do I owe you?" she asked, and held her breath.

Deke gave her a crooked smile. Despite knowing he was begging for trouble, he suggested, "Feed me dinner and we'll call it even."

Wary, Mary Beth studied him, irritated at the way her heart did a little flipflop at the thought of being with him for a while longer. But she didn't want his charity. "I can pay you."

"I didn't say you couldn't." He moved away from the wall and toward her, close enough to smell her scent, far enough to resist the temptation of kissing her. "So how about dinner? Sounds like it's raining pretty hard now, so I thought I'd wait around until it slacks off before I go." It was a thin excuse to stay with her.

"I don't know what I have," she answered honestly, then mentally ran through her cupboards. Unable to afford much more than the bare essentials, she hadn't been to the grocery store this week.

Deke shrugged. "It doesn't matter. I'm not picky. Would you mind if I took a quick shower?" Before she could protest, he whipped off his dirty shirt.

Mary Beth's mouth went dry at the sight of him half-naked. His skin was tanned, his shoulders strong and hard muscled, his chest lightly sprinkled with fine, dark blond hair. Her gaze devoured him, slipping down his flat stomach, stopping momentarily at his belt, then drifting dangerously lower to his hips.

She caught her breath. Long ago on the night they'd made love, she'd had the freedom to touch him intimately, to run her hands all over his body. Oh, my, she wished she could touch him now.

"Um, no, of course not," she said in a rush, diverting her gaze. "Maybe I can find you a clean shirt."

"Great. Don't start dinner until I'm out, so I can help," he warned. He turned and disappeared down the hall.

A moment later the bathroom door closed, and she heard the shower come on.

She stood. Her legs trembled and her heart pounded. It was all Mary Beth could do to make her way to her father's bedroom.

You can handle this, she told herself.

No, she couldn't. Deke was *naked* in *her* shower!

"Just keep your distance," she muttered as she entered her father's room. The musty smell, the faint yet familiar scent of her father, caused her footsteps to momentarily falter. She glanced around the room. Unpleasant memories came rushing back at her. Her father's disappointment in having a daughter, his criticism every time she tried to help with jobs on the ranch—and her burning desire to get away.

In two years she'd rarely entered his room, and now she was ready to rummage through her father's clothing for a shirt for Deke.

Deke! Getting her mind back on track, Mary Beth pulled open a dresser drawer. Snatching up a long-sleeved white shirt, she slammed the drawer shut and headed out of the room.

She approached the bathroom door with a mixture of hesitation and excitement. Should she leave the shirt outside the door, or open it and toss it in?

She could just go inside.

Go inside! Are you crazy?

Maybe, but if she went in just for a second, she'd be able to see the image of his nude body through the clouded glass shower door.

Oh, how she wanted to.

Badly.

She grasped the doorknob. *You shouldn't. It's an invasion of his privacy! Not to mention rude,* she chided herself. Her whole body shook with need and anticipation.

What *would* Deke think if she walked in? If she stripped off her clothes and offered herself to him? Could she do it? Could she start an affair with Deke, knowing there would never be more between them? Did she want to risk hurting her heart once again?

Soon, maybe even tomorrow, he would be leaving. Would it make a difference if she made love with him? She was leaving Crockett anyway, wasn't she?

But she couldn't bring herself to open the door.

Her pulse accelerated as she leaned closer, then pressed her cheek against the cool wood. Her eyelids drifted down, and she breathed deeply, her lungs filling almost painfully as she let her imagination run wild.

Drifting in a dream-filled state, she saw herself opening the door and stepping inside the small bathroom. Stripping out of her clothes with seductive intent, she stepped lightly across the room and reached for the metal handle of the glass door. Slowly, her heart pounding, she drew it open and stood wantonly naked before him. In her mind she took pleasure in the way Deke's blue eyes widened with surprise, then darkened with desire as his body hardened, readying itself for her.

Having never bathed with a man, the creative illusion of water cascading down their bare skin sparked an urgent need in the most intimate part of her body. Her breathing escalated as she envisioned herself in his arms, her full breasts brushing against his hard chest...

"Oh!" she squealed as the door abruptly swung open. Mary Beth fell forward and slammed against Deke's bare chest. The exquisite contact stole her breath. Startled, she stared aghast at his face. Lord help her, she'd been so lost in her fantasy that she hadn't even heard him turn off the water!

Deke's arms went around her, catching her fully against him. "Whoa."

"I was, um, bringing you a shirt," she blurted, tightening her hold on the garment now squashed between them. Heat rushed to her cheeks.

"I like your mode of delivery," he murmured, but he wasn't smiling. His eyes, heavy-lidded and hot with desire, drifted to her mouth.

She stilled with anticipation, knowing she was a fool to invite the intimacy of his kiss but unable to resist the temptation. Her mouth opened with silent invitation. Deke lowered his head, and his lips hovered above hers. Their breath mingled in what seemed like forever before he finally covered her mouth.

The pleasure of his lips, of his tongue sweeping into her mouth coursed through her, and Mary Beth moaned. Overwhelmed by her desire for Deke, she trembled in his arms, feeling the heady force of his kiss all the way to her toes. And the erotic smell of him—pure male, mixed with her own lavender-scented soap—filled her senses. She grasped his upper arms in a desperate attempt to keep her balance, then went up on her toes as his tongue made another slow, deliberate foray into her mouth.

Sinfully delicious.

Her resolve to keep him at a distance deserted her. His skin, still damp from his shower, was hot and moist beneath her palms. Pressed tightly against him, she could feel him harden. Her breasts swelled, her nipples ached as his hand drifted ever so slowly down her back, then lower still to cup her bottom. He cradled her body against his hips.

Suddenly he lifted his lips. Mary Beth instantly felt deprived of the pleasure of his mouth. She tensed, knowing what to expect. Her heart sank as she waited for him to bolt. In a moment he'd be running out the door, just as he'd done last night, just as he'd done two years ago.

"I promised myself that I could keep things between us platonic, but if you keep kissing me like that—" He broke off his sentence with a groan.

The burning intensity in his gaze made her pulse speed as cool air made contact with her wet lips. She could still taste him, and her knees went weak. Despite her resolve to keep her emotions under tight control, she wanted to mold herself against him.

Until now she'd hidden her attraction to him. After the kiss they'd shared last night, he'd left so suddenly that she felt he had no idea that she'd been half in love with him all of her life.

Before she could gather her wits, Deke did something that totally took her breath away. He tightened his arms around her and hugged her close as he rested his chin on her head. His breathing, hard and labored, mimicked hers.

"Honey, if I was staying in Crockett, I'd take you down to the floor and pleasure you until you begged me to come inside you." His guttural tone left no doubt that he meant what he said.

Mary Beth didn't tell him that she was only moments from doing just that. To have him admit his desire for her blew her mind. To have him hold her and touch her, make love to her, would be ecstasy.

It would also be lethal to your heart.

She shook her head. Instead of dreaming about an affair with Deke, which had no place to go, she should be glad that he'd had the presence of mind to stop things before they'd gone too far. Her feelings for him already ran too deep.

"Promises, promises," she teased, her voice husky. Intent on getting her bearings, she moved out of his arms and gave him the wrinkled shirt. Before she could put more distance between them, he snagged her hand.

"I'm staying." He waited until her eyes met his, then quietly looked at her a long moment. "For dinner," he added with a taut look, then began shrugging into the shirt.

Mary Beth nodded. Her heartbeat quickened as she led the way to the kitchen. Trying to get her mind on food and off how much she wanted to kiss Deke, she began searching for something to prepare. Deke had already rummaged through her understocked cabinets, so he was well aware that there wasn't much to choose from.

Opening the freezer door, she peered inside and inspected the contents. "I think I have some steaks," she told him, relieved when she found several shrink-wrapped packages. Clyde had preferred to keep to his own company, which had been perfectly fine with her, so she rarely bothered to cook just for herself. She turned toward him, avoiding his eyes. "If we broil them slowly, they'll defrost as they cook."

"Sounds great."

"Do you like rice?" She said a silent prayer that he did. When he nodded, she breathed a relieved sigh, knowing she didn't have anything else to fix with the steaks if he'd said no. "I have a wonderful recipe for rice and black beans. I can make it while the steaks broil," she said as she got two glasses and filled them with ice and tea.

Mindful of her nervousness, Deke took the steaks from

her. When he'd kissed her, she'd been just as turned on as him. Interesting. "I'll take care of the steaks while you get the rice and beans started." Maybe it was foolish to hang around and torture himself by being near her and keeping his hands off her, but he couldn't bring himself to leave.

Mary Beth nodded, then retrieved a pan for him to use and handed it to him. Trying to ease the tension, she asked, "So, how are you doing on the rodeo circuit?" She'd heard bits and pieces of his bull-riding exploits over the past two years. Each little detail had interested her.

He shrugged, not allowing himself to read anything other than idle curiosity into her question. "I do okay."

She stopped in the process of opening a box of rice and put a hand on her hip. "Oh, c'mon. There was an article in the paper only a few weeks ago that reported you're the front-runner." She'd heard he had five major companies backing him. That alone told her he was one of the best.

He frowned. Did he notice a trace of sarcasm in her tone? Deke was used to the good-natured teasing of his brothers. Though they got on his case about being fool-hardy, he could still see the pride in their eyes. He'd even gotten used to Catherine and Ashley fussing over him, making him promise to wear a protective vest. For a reason he couldn't explain, he wanted to know what Mary Beth thought. Did she think he was irresponsible? Did she care what happened to him? Or did she think he was crazy for spending his time on the back of a bull? "Yeah," was all he said with a shrug.

She hid a smile. Surprised by his reluctance to talk about his exploits, she watched him. "Well, first place is pretty cool, huh?"

Deke slid the steaks into the oven. "I'm in front. That doesn't mean I'll stay there. A bad ride for me, a good ride for a competitor, and I'm the one behind. That's why

I have to get to Houston tomorrow. There's two other guys on my butt," he went on. "If I don't show up, my standings will slip. They may, anyway, if I don't perform well." And he wouldn't if he didn't get Mary Beth off his mind, which wasn't likely because he'd been hard as a rock since he'd kissed her.

He should just leave. What was he thinking of, staying here?

"What's it like?" She added the rice to boiling water, then covered the pot with a lid and turned the heat down. "I mean, riding a bull?" she asked, taking a sip of her tea.

He cocked his head, his grin mischievous as amusement danced in his eyes. "Unbelievable. The adrenaline rush is almost as good as sex."

Mary Beth nearly choked on the liquid in her throat. She shot him a warning look. "Behave or I'll send you home hungry." Her hands were shaking, but somehow she managed to open a can of black beans without spilling them all over the counter. She took a bowl out of a cabinet and dumped the beans in it. "Why do you ride?" It couldn't be money, she thought. With one of the most profitable ranches in Texas, the McCalls were surely wealthy. "Is it the prestige?"

He shook his head, but his distant manner at the mention of the rodeo piqued her curiosity. She pushed the subject, wanting to know more about him. "I've always wondered what makes a man live so dangerously." Her contempt for footloose, danger-seeking rodeo cowboys was revealed in her tone. She'd always thought of them as shallow and reckless, living only for each thrilling competition, not caring about anyone but themselves and the wild ride.

Was that really true? Deke had proven to be just the opposite, hadn't he? He was caring and gentle and seemed genuinely concerned about her. When he easily could have left, he'd stayed with her to make sure she was okay, had stayed around to help her.

"I don't think about the danger."

He was checking the steaks, and she couldn't see his face. The sexual tension that had built between them had eased somewhat, making conversation more tolerable.

"How did you get started? Did you always want to be a rodeo cowboy?" She added spices and salsa to the beans.

"I was always fascinated by bull riding, and I started bugging my dad about letting me compete. When he felt I was old enough, he let me begin training." Shaking his head, he smiled, but there was an unmistakable sadness in his eyes. "Until his death, he never missed a competition." His heart ached for the days before his father had died, when he'd been the son Jacob McCall had been proud of.

"But *why* do you still do it?" she asked again, feeling there was something he wasn't saying. "You take a chance on getting killed every time you climb on the back of a bull." Remaining silent, he watched her check the rice, then turn the burner off. She pushed him further. "You've been hurt in the competitions before, haven't you?"

He shrugged. "There's an element of danger, yeah." He went on talking, describing some of his rides and telling her of his injuries, dismissing broken bones and torn ligaments as if they were no more than scratches.

Mary Beth knew differently. She'd heard stories about Deke returning home and recuperating from injuries he'd sustained during competition. Her heart twisted. Didn't he know he could be hurt permanently, maybe never walk again, if a bull threw him and stomped on him—or worse, killed him? The thought of such an accident occurring, of his beautiful body twisted and scarred for life, made her cringe.

Deke looked up at that moment and saw the anguish and concern in her expression. For him. Overwhelmed, a cold place in his heart warmed at the thought of Mary Beth caring about what happened to him.

Other than Ashley and Catherine, no other woman had shown such concern for him. He'd treated Mary Beth badly in the past, and he didn't deserve her compassion. She should hate him for having walked out on her two years ago.

"How long are you gonna ride, Deke?" she asked. "How long are you going to take a chance on getting killed?"

Shaken by the sincerity of her question, he looked away. "As long as it takes to win the championship." He leaned down to check the steaks, then took them out of the oven as she stirred the bean mixture into the rice.

Blowing out a frustrated breath, she filled two plates with rice and beans, added the steaks, then carried them to the table. "Why is that so important?" She didn't understand. What drove him? Didn't he care about himself, about those who loved him?

His recklessness struck her as odd. He cared about his family, loved them enough to come home to visit as often as possible, but he continued to risk his life in a competition that would bring him nothing more than some prestige and a gold belt buckle.

"I want to win the championship before I'm too old to compete."

They sat at the table. She regarded him with more than just casual curiosity. "You're hardly old," she remarked, cutting a small bite of steak. "Only a couple of years older than me, and I'll be twenty-six on Thursday." Mary Beth gasped, stunned that she'd blurted she was having a birthday. To her acute embarrassment, Deke jumped right on it.

He winked, then forked a piece of steak in his mouth. "Twenty-six, huh?" His gaze centered on her face. "This Thursday?"

Upset that she'd slipped and mentioned her birthday, she looked away. "It's no big deal. Just another day." And it would be, she thought, sadness creeping over her. As had been in most of her adult life, there would be no one special to celebrate with. Since her mother had died, her birthday, as well as holidays like Thanksgiving and Christmas, meant that she'd be alone while others gathered together with families and loved ones. She had no one.

It was a fact of life she'd learned to live with.

Mary Beth became quiet as she finished eating, and Deke wondered why the mention of her birthday brought such a dispirited expression in her eyes. He shoved his empty plate away. She deserved to spend her birthday celebrating, not alone.

"There's more rice," Mary Beth said when she noticed he'd finished eating.

Deke chuckled and patted his full stomach. "It was delicious, but I'm stuffed." He checked his watch, then shoved his chair away from the table. "What are you trying to do? Fatten me up so I'm too big to ride?"

She smiled, and her eyes brightened as she looked at him. "Would it work?"

"I know what I'm doing," he said, his eyes serious.

Realizing he was leaving, she stood and took their plates to the sink. She wiped her hands on a towel, then turned to face him, trying very hard not to show how much she'd enjoyed his company. "If you say so."

His gaze drifted lazily over her, and the itch he had to take her to bed was back in an instant, followed by a deep desire to keep her there for a week. ''I'd better get home and pack.''

She nodded, then followed him as he walked to the front door. He snatched his hat from the rack where he'd hung it earlier, then opened the door and stepped outside. He turned to take one last look at her.

Mary Beth had followed him out onto the porch. ''Thanks for everything.'' The rain hadn't let up. Lightning crackled and streaked across the night sky. Wrapping her arms around herself, she said, ''You could stay until it lets up.'' Despite the intimacy of their kiss, he hadn't touched her again. But, oh, how she wanted him to.

Deke was sorely tempted to stay with her. His loins ached, and he could think of nothing more enjoyable than to satisfy his lust by burying himself deep inside of her. But he couldn't use her. Over the past two days, she'd come to mean more than just an easy roll in the hay. And he had to leave before she meant more.

''I have to go.''

Did that mean that he had to get to the rodeo, or that he had to get away from her? Mary Beth looked away.

Deke watched as her expression grew somber. His gut tightened with the need to take care of her, to drive that hurt look from her expression. Unable to stop himself, he reached for her. She came willingly into his arms, pressing close to him, burying her face against his chest. Her arms slid around his waist and tightened.

''Take care of yourself,'' she whispered, then started to pull away.

Deke held her to him. She lifted her face to look up at him, her eyes softening, her cheeks rosy. ''I'm going to kiss you goodbye,'' he said, and watched as the sadness in her eyes grew to desire. Her lips parted as he lowered his mouth and took hers with an almost desperate hunger.

The gratification was so unbelievably powerful that Deke groaned. His need to taste her one last time surpassed his will to keep his feelings for her under tight control. He deepened the kiss as she clung to him. Hot, aching for her, he explored her mouth with his tongue, and her moist warmth enveloped him. Her soft, delicate moan of pleasure made his blood hot.

He could feel her breasts pressed against him, and his hand moved to cup one, finding her nipple hardened to a rigid peak. He caressed her with his fingers, and she pressed her hips against the cradle of his pelvis, against the hard bulge in his jeans, driving him close to the edge of insanity.

Deke tore his mouth from hers. This was wrong. If he didn't stop things between them now, he wouldn't be able to walk away from her. His breathing was rough, his chest heaving as he sucked in air. He tightened his arms around her for a brief moment, then let her go, stepping quickly away from her while he still could.

He had to leave. Now. Mary Beth wasn't the type of woman for a quick tumble. And a quickie with her wouldn't come close to satisfying this overwhelming need he had for her.

His gaze, heavy-lidded with desire, swept slowly over her. Her eyes were glistening, her lips swollen from his kiss.

Go, he ordered himself. Forcing himself to move, he turned and made his way to his truck, immune to the pelting rain and mighty roar of thunder.

Her heart pounding, Mary Beth stared after Deke, watched him walk out of her life.

Just like two years ago.

No, not exactly. This time she hadn't slept with him.

You wanted to.

Oh, yeah, she did. But his leaving was best. She knew it was. Somehow, he'd begun to tear down her defenses, to make her want him again. She'd made the mistake of trusting her heart to Deke before. Watching him leave hurt her, but the pain was far less than it would have been if she let herself fall in love with him.

Again.

Six

In the quiet of the early morning, Mary Beth lay in her bed and stared at the ceiling, the empty house closing in on her. Sunlight began peeking through her drab beige curtains as silence enveloped her. The isolation, the complete aloneness, was almost too much to bear.

It's only your birthday. You should be used to spending the day alone.

Though she'd made casual friends while living and working in San Antonio, none of them had been close enough to even know the date of her birthday, let alone take time out of their busy schedule to celebrate it with her.

She sniffed and touched a finger to her face where a single tear trickled down her cheek. She really had to shake these blues. It was a waste of time feeling sorry for herself.

Is it company you miss? Or Deke?

Deke.

She didn't miss Deke McCall, but even as she denied the thought, his handsome face drifted through her mind. He'd only been gone five days. Five days! She balled her fists and closed her eyes. Why was she lying here thinking about Deke?

She didn't need a man in her life, didn't *want* a man in her life. Hadn't she learned the hard way that men couldn't be trusted, couldn't be depended on? Her father had been a prime example. Hank Adams had never been around when she and her mother had needed him. Instead of supporting them both during her mother's illness, her father had run off chasing another of his foolish schemes to get rich quick.

She didn't need a man.

Especially a man like Deke McCall, whose ambition in life was to win some stupid rodeo title.

He's already proved to you that he couldn't be depended on.

"You should be thanking your lucky stars that he's gone," she chided herself as she opened her eyes and forced herself to get out of bed, "instead of pining for him like some silly teenager." She'd be a fool to let him close enough to hurt her again. And the best way to make sure that didn't happen was to stop thinking about him.

Easier said than done, when all she thought about was the way she'd felt in his arms. And how much, against every sane thought, she'd wanted to kiss him again.

Fatigued from a rough night's sleep and from doing all of the daily ranch chores alone, she trudged to the bathroom, every muscle in her body begging for a massage. Her days were long and hard, and she'd pushed herself to the point of exhaustion just trying to keep up. Each day it was getting more difficult to get everything done.

Even she had been forced to admit to herself that there

was no way she could continue running the ranch without help. So, two days ago, she'd placed an advertisement in the paper for a ranch hand. But it was a foolish waste of time. She could only pay minimum wage. Who in their right mind would work for that small amount of money? Though she silently prayed someone would, if she never received one phone call, she wouldn't be surprised.

She blew out a breath. If she could just hang on, keep things going until she sold her herd, she'd be able to make the mortgage. That would give her a bit of breathing space. Not much, but some.

After a quick shower she brushed her teeth and dressed, then headed for the kitchen. A couple of cups of hot coffee and a bowl of oatmeal later, she stepped out of the house onto the front porch. The ground was finally drying from three straight days of rain. Her boots left slight imprints in soft dirt as she drudged across the yard.

Entering the barn, she came to an abrupt halt. Every time she saw the hay stacked high against the wall in the barn, she thought of Deke. No wonder she couldn't get the man off her mind! When he'd bargained with her for dinner, she'd had no idea of how much hay and feed he'd purchased. She'd intended on sending him a check immediately, but at the end of each day, she'd been too darn tired to make the effort. Today she'd take care of it!

She fed the horses, turned them into the corral, then began cleaning their stalls. She was just about done when she heard the distant sound of a truck approaching.

Her eyebrows dipping, she put down her rake and pulled off her gloves. As she walked out of the barn, she shaded her eyes from the glare of the sun. Looking in the direction of the driveway as she headed toward the front of her house, she blinked, then suddenly stopped in her tracks.

Deke! Heavens, she'd just been thinking about him! Paralyzed, Mary Beth watched as his truck rolled into the yard and parked near the front of the house.

He got out of the truck and called her name.

What was he doing here? Her heartbeat accelerated at the sight of him. It nearly tripled its rate as he came around the truck in that slow, deliberate pace she was coming to recognize.

Sexy. Oh, yeah.

Trouble to her heart.

Definitely.

Trying to recapture her composure, she stuffed her shaking hands into the pockets of her jeans, unwilling to let him see how excited she was to see him.

Then she saw them. Two black-and-white blurs of energy bounding out of his truck, barking with excitement as they raced toward her. She grinned. Kneeling down, she greeted the spirited dogs.

"Hey, there!" The two animals competed with each other for her attention. She patted both dogs on their heads, then ran her hands lovingly over their glossy coats. "Oh, you're so sweet."

"If I got a greeting like that when I came to see you, I think I'd have to come by more often," Deke remarked. He stopped in front of Mary Beth, his grin wide enough to show his straight, white teeth.

"Oh, yeah?" she answered, looking up at him, her eyebrows raised. "I guess I'll have to work on my greeting skills, huh?" Her spine tingled as his gaze dropped to her mouth. Though he was teasing her, the thought of greeting him with a kiss was awfully tempting.

"You can start now if you want." He spread his arms wide, as if offering himself as a sacrifice.

She couldn't help but smile. "I didn't say I'd practice on *you*," she replied sweetly. Deke frowned, and she was a little pleased with herself for not giving in to his flirting. She didn't know why he was here, but there was one thing she knew for sure. He wasn't staying.

Still patting the dogs, she looked up at him. "What are you doing here?" she asked, changing the subject before it moved to dangerous ground. "And who are your friends?"

Deke crouched beside her. One of the dogs immediately came to him, eager for more attention. "They're great, aren't they?" he remarked.

He hadn't expected to come back to see Mary Beth at all, but he hadn't been able to get her off his mind. Though he hadn't come in first at the rodeo, he'd scored well enough to stay in the lead in total points. His last night there, he'd spotted a young couple outside the arena, with three small kids and two dogs. The kids had been holding a sign, offering the herding dogs free to a good home.

Curious, Deke had struck up a conversation with them and had learned they were moving and couldn't take the animals along. Deke had immediately thought of Mary Beth's situation, and before he could stop himself, he'd offered to take the dogs. His mission to bring the dogs to her had been altruistic. It bothered him that she was alone and had to work so hard.

But the moment he'd seen her crossing the yard and coming toward him, his libido had kicked into high gear. All he could think about was what was hidden beneath those tight jeans and that baggy T-shirt. She looked even better than he remembered. And the huge smile on her face made him feel that the trip was worth the time it took out of his schedule.

"They sure are." She wrinkled her nose when one long, pink tongue licked her cheek.

Deke looked the dog in the eye. "Sit." Both dogs sat

in unison, their mouths open, their eyes alert. "This one is Lightning," he told Mary Beth. "See, he has a white lightning streak on his head." He nodded toward the other dog. "And that's Lady."

Both dogs were mostly black, with white patches of fur. They also had white fur on their feet, and their tails had a white tip. "They're border collies, aren't they?" She looked at Deke for confirmation and found him watching her. "They're absolutely gorgeous. But I thought border collies had long hair." The coats of Lightning and Lady were soft and much shorter than she'd seen on other dogs of the same breed.

"They're smooth border collies so their hair isn't as long or thick," he explained.

"Oh." She watched the dogs a minute. Both of their tails were wagging, making semicircles in the dirt as they dragged the ground.

Deke gave her a grin and winked. "I was hoping you'd like them."

Mary Beth's eyes locked with his. "You were?"

He nodded and stood, then waited for her to do the same. Once upright, she turned toward him, her expression curious.

"Happy Birthday."

"What?" She stared at him, and her mouth dropped open.

"Today is your birthday," he reminded her. "You didn't forget, did you?"

Forget? Stunned, Mary Beth very slowly shook her head. Deke was there because he'd remembered her birthday? "No, but—"

"Well, I didn't, either." Deke explained about how he met the dogs' owners at the rodeo. "They didn't want to leave them behind, but felt since they been raised on a ranch, they wouldn't be happy in the city."

She frowned, still trying to comprehend what he was saying. "Oh, how sad."

"I felt bad for them, but they were relieved when I told him I'd make sure they were taken care of. The kids seemed especially happy to know they were going to a good home."

"It must've been really hard for them."

"It was, but I assured them that the dogs were perfect for you."

Still reeling from the shock of Deke making a special trip there for her birthday, she shook her head. "You came all the way back to bring them to me? For my birthday?" Tears filled her eyes. It had been years since her birthday meant more than going through the motions of the day, then coming home to spend it alone.

He cleared his throat. "Well, yeah." That and he couldn't stay away, couldn't get her out of his mind. And now that he was here, he wanted to do a whole lot more than just look at her.

Mary Beth suppressed the desire to cry and focused on the dogs. Worry creased a line between her eyes. "It was a very sweet thing to do, Deke. Really, I appreciate it. But, I can't take these dogs in right now." It broke her heart just thinking about letting them go. "I have my hands full keeping this place up."

She looked at the two dogs, who were still sitting side by side, eagerly looking at her with chocolate-brown eyes, begging for attention. The aching feeling in her chest accelerated. Her funds were already low. How could she afford to care for two dogs, as well?

Deke could see that she was already half in love with the dogs. "Do you know anything about border collies?"

"Not a lot," she admitted. "I know they're smart. I heard somewhere that they're the whiz kids of dog breeds."

Deke grabbed her hand and started tugging her toward the corral. "Lightning, Lady!" The dogs were already at their heels before he'd finished speaking.

"Where are we going?" She tried to pull her hand free. His touch was doing crazy things to her insides. But he didn't let her go until they were at the fence.

"Watch," he said, then he left her and led the two dogs inside the corral with the horses. "I'm gonna show you how much you're gonna love these two."

Mary Beth knew that wouldn't take much. She was already falling for the darling creatures and could just imagine how much company they'd be for her. But even without the monetary aspect, she really didn't have the time or energy the two dogs would require, no matter how tempting they were to keep.

As Deke entered the corral with the dogs, she stood at the fence, her eyes glued to the three of them. The horses began moving about from the sudden disruption. Deke called out to the dogs, who began moving about inside the corral. Within minutes Mary Beth was fascinated by watching the animals work.

Using a series of spoken commands and hand signals, Lightning and Lady started working, herding the horses, bringing them together in the center of the corral. They took their job seriously, darting back and forth until the horses were herded together in short order. Then, at another command, they crouched low and guarded their prey.

"They're working dogs," Deke called to Mary Beth. "They'll herd just about anything, and they're gonna help you herd your cattle."

Mary Beth was speechless. She'd heard of the ability of

herding dogs before, but she'd never seen one of them at work. Finding her voice, she said, "Oh, my! I can't believe they can do that." They were so smart. And absolutely adorable. And Deke was sweet to have brought them to her. She'd have to spend money on their food, but they'd be worth it ten times over by helping to herd the cattle.

And would be a lot more dependable than a man.

"You'll have to be careful that they don't work too hard," Deke warned, looking at the sun, then back at her. "C'mon guys," he called to the dogs, and slapped his hand against his thigh. Moving at what seemed like warp speed, they shot toward him, anxiously prancing around his legs. He gave both dogs a caress. "They love what they do, and sometimes they don't know when to quit."

Deke exited the corral with the dogs and shut the gate. "The commands they know are easy enough to learn. I'll teach you. They already know what their job is, so you won't even have to tell them most of the time. You just need to know when and how to call them to you so they'll learn that you're in charge." He looked expectantly at Mary Beth. "So, what do you think?"

"I don't know what to say. I mean, I can't believe you did this." Overwhelmed by his kindness, her throat tightened as she came up to him. She reached her hand out to touch him, then stopped herself, unwilling to trust her emotions.

It had been a long time since anyone had shown her such kindness. She was torn between laughing and crying.

He shrugged. "They needed a home on a ranch, and you needed some help. It seemed like a perfect match. They'll be company for you, as well," he added, as if to convince her. "You're pretty isolated out here."

Mary Beth brushed a wisp of hair behind her ear as she stepped closer to him, telling herself not to read anything into his good deed. "It must've been out of your way to come here."

"I was headed to the next rodeo in Lubbock," he said, as if it was on his way. He started for his truck, then turned and waited for her to join him before he began walking again. As if they'd received a command, the dogs followed along. "I stopped and bought them some food. I didn't know when you'd get a chance to get away."

His thoughtfulness shouldn't have surprised Mary Beth. She was discovering that Deke wasn't as carefree and reckless as she'd believed. "I still owe you for the supplies you picked up before you left. I'll write you a check for all of it before you go."

Deke shot her a frown as he reached his truck, picked up a huge sack of dog food from the bed, and hoisted it up on his shoulder. "We've already settled that. You fed me dinner, remember?"

Mary Beth stared at him in fascination, watching as his muscles bunched and worked as he settled the sack on his shoulder. She had to tear her gaze away from his body. "That hardly repays you for the money you spent. I had no idea at the time how much you'd bought." As she was talking, he'd turned and started for the house. She quickly followed, trying to keep up with his longer stride.

"A deal's a deal," he called over his shoulder. "I'll put this on the back porch."

Mary Beth rushed to beat him to the door so she could hold it for him. They went inside, Lightning and Lady following as if they'd done it all of their lives. Deke lowered the dog food to the floor, then turned to face her.

"So, are you gonna keep 'em?" He made himself at home by opening the door from the porch to the house and walking inside.

Mary Beth and the dogs followed him. The two animals

checked out the new surroundings, then they disappeared from view. "Looks like they're already making themselves at home."

"Is that a yes?"

She nodded, then tilted her head slightly, her eyes glistening with unshed tears as her throat tightened with emotion. "Thank you, Deke. I can't remember the last time anyone even remembered my birthday, let alone gave me a gift." A lone tear rolled down her cheek. She hadn't meant to cry, but his generosity and thoughtfulness destroyed her defenses. Embarrassed, she wiped the tear away with the back of her hand.

Deke couldn't stop himself from touching her. His hand went to the back of her head, his fingers in her hair. His thumb caressed the delicate skin of her neck. "I didn't mean to make you cry."

"It's not you," she assured him. Standing only inches away, she could feel his body heat. Her own temperature went up a few degrees. "I mean, it is, but not..." She bit her lip, hesitated and then, as if was the most natural thing in the world to do, she moved toward him. Her palms rested against his chest as she brushed his lips with hers. "Thank you."

She started to move away, but his arm slipped around her back and held her to him. All of her senses went on alert. She was keenly aware of his masculinity, of how much she wanted, needed to be in his arms.

He tilted her face up, his gaze intense. "You're welcome," he murmured. He stared at her silently, holding himself in check.

Mary Beth knew what he wanted; she wanted the same thing. Despite all the warnings she'd given herself about getting further involved with Deke, she wanted nothing more at this moment than to make love with him.

He sighed. "I didn't come back here to seduce you."

"You didn't?" His blunt words seared her heart. She stared at him, her eyes questioning. Had she misread his intentions? Pink color tinged her cheeks.

"I can get sex anytime I want it," he told her. He cupped her chin with his hand.

"Oh." She stiffened and tried to move away, but his arm was like a steel band, holding her to him.

"I don't want to hurt you, Mary Beth."

A sigh escaped her lips as understanding dawned on her. He wanted her sexually, but as before, would leave the moment they were finished making love. She appreciated his honesty, but she hadn't really expected anything more from him.

His thumb slid across her mouth. Mary Beth parted her lips. She touched his thumb with the tip of her tongue and watched a blazing fire light his eyes. "It's okay," she whispered. This was her birthday, and this time she didn't want to spend it alone. She deserved to be happy tonight, didn't she? Being with Deke would fill the loneliness inside her. It didn't have to mean anything more. If she sacrificed her pride, wouldn't it be worth it for even a few intimate hours alone with him?

Her breathing became rapid as he lowered his head and kissed her. Burrowing closer, she pressed against the hard length of him. Her nipples tightened to a pleasurable ache as he spread his legs and settled her between them. A groan of sheer pleasure escaped her lips. He lifted his mouth, and she gasped for air before he covered it again, kissing her deeply. His tongue slid into her mouth, increasing the desire raging deep within her core.

"I want to be inside you," Deke said roughly, his voice strained.

There was a desperation in his voice Mary Beth hadn't

Get FREE BOOKS and a FREE GIFT when you play the...

LAS VEGAS

GAME

Just scratch off the gold box with a coin. Then check below to see the gifts you get!

YES! I have scratched off the gold Box. Please send me my **2 FREE BOOKS** and **gift for which I qualify.** I understand that I am under no obligation to purchase any books as explained on the back of this card.

326 SDL DRQE   **225 SDL DRQU**

FIRST NAME	LAST NAME

ADDRESS

APT.#	CITY

(S-D-12/02)

STATE/PROV.	ZIP/POSTAL CODE

7	7	7	Worth TWO FREE BOOKS plus a BONUS Mystery Gift!
🍒	🍒	🍒	Worth TWO FREE BOOKS!
🔔	🔔	☘	TRY AGAIN!

Visit us online at
www.eHarlequin.com

Offer limited to one per household and not valid to current Silhouette Desire® subscribers. All orders subject to approval.

The Silhouette Reader Service™ — Here's how it works:

Accepting your 2 free books and mystery gift places you under no obligation to buy anything. You may keep the books and gift and return the shipping statement marked "cancel." If you do not cancel, about a month later we'll send you 6 additional books and bill you just $3.57 each in the U.S., or $4.24 each in Canada, plus 25¢ shipping & handling per book and applicable taxes if any.* That's the complete price and — compared to cover prices of $4.25 each in the U.S. and $4.99 each in Canada — it's quite a bargain! You may cancel at any time, but if you choose to continue, every month we'll send you 6 more books, which you may either purchase at the discount price or return to us and cancel your subscription.

*Terms and prices subject to change without notice. Sales tax applicable in N.Y. Canadian residents will be charged applicable provincial taxes and GST.

expected. It made her move more fully against him. His hands sought her buttocks and lifted her against him.

They both groaned.

Deke yanked Mary Beth's shirt out of her jeans, shoving it up and out of his way, then pulling it over her head. Her hair cascaded down around her creamy shoulders as he reached behind her and released the catch on her white cotton bra.

"I've seen you like this a million times in my mind," he murmured. His mouth moved with erotic skill across her skin.

Before Mary Beth could digest his staggering confession, his tongue traced a scorching path to her nipple. Leaning her over his arm, he suckled her, giving equal attention to both breasts. Her eyes slid closed. The roughness of his tongue was so exquisite, so incredibly wonderful that she trembled in his arms. Her bones seemed to melt from the heat building between her legs.

Deke scooped her into his arms, kissing her as he made his way to her room. He wanted her in her bed, wanted to make love to her until he had his fill. Maybe then he could get his mind on the rodeo.

In her room he shoved the door shut with his shoulder, then laid her gently on the bed. Mary Beth stared up at him as he unbuttoned his shirt and pulled it off. Hungry for the taste of her, he leaned over her and kissed her hard. She wound her arms around his neck, pulling him down to her. Deke grunted with satisfaction as her breasts grazed his chest.

Still kissing her, he made short work of the clasp and zipper of her jeans. He slid his hand inside her panties as his mouth continued to plunder hers. She was wet, her body already responding to his lovemaking.

She accepted his fingers, then began moving her hips

against his hand, her body taking over as a wave of ecstasy swept everything from her mind except how absolutely perfect it felt to be with him. He continued to pleasure her as he removed her boots, then tugged her jeans and panties off.

"Hurry," she whispered, her voice soft and pleading.

"I am," he said huskily, and yanked off his boots. His jeans quickly followed. He couldn't take his eyes off her. Seeing her lying on the bed, beautifully naked and staring at him, her eyes heavy lidded with desire, was almost more than he could take. She was so hot, so ready for him, that he almost forgot to protect her. He quickly found the packet in his wallet, sheathed himself, then moved over her and nudged her legs apart.

As he entered her, she welcomed him into her with a soft sigh, then slowly began moving against him. Her body gloved his perfectly, too perfectly, as if she were made just for him.

At that moment Deke knew he would never be the same again. But it was too late to turn back, too late to save himself from her. He needed her, needed to see her go crazy for him. He met her thrust for thrust, building her pleasure and his own. Her eyes drifted shut as she clung to him, her fingers digging into his flesh as she began to peak. Grasping her buttocks, he drove deeper, harder into her. When she cried out his name, Deke gritted his teeth and joined her in a world of ecstasy.

A short while later as she lay in his arms, Mary Beth felt him stir. She opened her eyes. He would leave her now, as he always did. Her arms were still locked around him, holding him to her. Her chest began to ache as she let them fall to her side, freeing him to go.

She had known this time would come, but despite expecting it, the thought of him leaving brought bone-crushing pain. Forcing herself to accept reality, she looked at him.

Deke raised himself off her. He kissed her hungrily, then stared at her, his blue eyes intense. "I'm not leaving." He couldn't. Not yet. Not when he still wanted her with a desperation that he didn't even want to analyze.

He watched her for a moment, waiting until she gave a look of pure surprise. Her pupils became more focused as his words finally registered, and he tried hard to ignore the way that made him feel inside. She was absolutely beautiful, her face flushed from their lovemaking. He liked being the one who'd put that contented look in her eyes, that rosy flush on her skin. He had to tear himself away to get up and go into the bathroom.

Mary Beth had turned on her side when he left her, watching his magnificent naked body move with a mixture of simple grace and exquisite power. Though making love with him meant much more to her than it ever would to him, she couldn't regret it. What she needed was to try to distance herself.

But even that could wait awhile, she thought, as he joined her again, pulling her against his hard body and welcoming heat. She sighed with immense pleasure and snuggled closer. Touching her hands to his chest, she boldly slipped her leg between his, pressing her thigh against his sex.

Her head lay tucked under his chin, so she couldn't see his face, but his whole body tensed and he moaned and moved against her. Silence fell between them, and she lay there enjoying the intense pleasure of being with him. She was startled when he spoke.

"I'm sorry I left you so suddenly two years ago, sweetheart. I never meant to hurt you." His hand stroked her back, tracing the small bumps of her spine, then cupped her breast.

"It's okay." It wasn't at the time, of course, but she'd learned to live with his rejection. "This more than made up for it." She lifted her head up so she could see him and gave him a slow, shy smile. "Do you want to know why I slept with you then?" she asked quietly, then looked away.

He touched her chin, forcing her to look back at him. "I *know* why. You were vulnerable after your father's funeral, and I took advantage of you." His finger touched her nipple, and it hardened beneath his touch. Deke felt like a lucky man. He'd treated her badly in the past. He didn't deserve this time with her.

"Is that what you thought?" He gave her a grim nod. "It wasn't anything like that." She felt her face and neck flush as she went on, "I feel kind of silly telling you this, but you really should know the truth." She hadn't realized he'd felt guilty over the years. It didn't make up for her hurt, but she had more respect for him. "I had the biggest crush on you when we were young," she confessed, toying with the fine curls on his chest.

"You did?" Just thinking that she'd been infatuated with him made him hard again. He rolled her over on her back, then touched his mouth to one erect nipple. He bit it gently with his teeth, then looked up at her and enjoyed the passion that flared in her eyes.

"I used to dream of what it would be like to make love with you," she said softly. She wasn't surprised that he never knew. He'd had his pick of girls, had never looked at her twice. "When you kissed me that day, it was my chance to see if being with you was anything like I thought it would be."

"And was it?" Deke asked, turning his attention to her

other breast. He suckled her, drawing her deep into his mouth.

Mary Beth started to tell him exactly how she felt when he was making love to her—how she wanted so much for him to never stop. But she could never confess that intimate detail, could never tell him that at some point, her crush had changed to something much more profound. If she did, he'd leave her for sure.

She gave him a wicked grin. "I don't know. I'm still trying to make up my mind." Despite her words, she moaned pleasurably when he teased at her nipple with his hot tongue. Her back arched, and her hips moved against him.

"Well, sweetheart, it looks like you need more evidence," he muttered thickly, his groin becoming heavy with his own desire.

Mary Beth gasped when his mouth left her breasts and traced a path across her belly. Then he spread her legs and tasted her. Hardly able to breathe, she groaned deep in her throat, then wave after wave of pleasure began to build inside her body.

And she no longer remembered what they'd been talking about.

Seven

Contented, her naked body sprawled wantonly over Deke, Mary Beth sighed softly. His warm hand caressed her body, gliding across her dewy skin with a lover's gentle touch, sending a ripple of pleasure coursing through her. Taking a liberty she'd only dreamed of in the past, she pressed her lips against his chest. It felt so good to be in his arms.

Too good.

But she wasn't going to let herself think past this moment. She'd savor their time together, wouldn't worry about a future between them or if one even existed. But even as the thought crossed her mind, she felt him stir, and all of her emotional defenses went up. When she tried to move away, he rolled over, taking her with him. She looked up to find him watching her.

"What?" she asked, when he continued to study her.

Deke hesitated, then murmured, "Making love with you

is fantastic." He'd never felt like this with a woman—as if he couldn't get enough of her. Which scared him as much as it excited him. He couldn't afford to get side-tracked, couldn't allow Mary Beth to become important to him. Still, he couldn't seem to leave her. Not yet.

His admission drew a dreamy smile to her lips. To hear him admit that he enjoyed being with her made her tingle all over. "Mmm. It was wonderful, wasn't it?"

"Oh, yeah." Deke's stomach muscles tensed. She was passionate and sexy, and he was going to have a hell of a time walking away.

Watching his expression grow distant, she frowned. "Oh. I thought I heard a but. What is it?"

He sighed, suddenly not liking himself very much. "Mary Beth, I don't want to hurt you."

Her eyes became somber. "You'll hurt me more if you're not honest with me." She waited for him to speak, but she already knew what he was going to say.

"I'm not the kind of man you need."

A hand squeezed her heart. "And what kind of man is that?"

"The staying kind. The kind of man who can make you promises and keep them."

She lowered her lashes slightly, concealing the pain his words caused her. "I don't need a man, Deke," she answered quietly, trying to swallow past the lump in her throat. "Besides, I don't remember asking anything of you."

Deke ran his finger down her cheek, and her eyes met his. *Yet.* In his mind, he heard the unspoken word. Whether she wanted to admit it or not, eventually she would. And he wouldn't be there for her.

Again.

What was he doing? He'd hurt her once—and he would

hurt her again. He was destined to hurt the people he cared about. And he was beginning to care about Mary Beth far more than he should. Whatever was happening between them, it was making his life pure hell. He blew out a breath. "Maybe not. I didn't stay with you before because I didn't have anything to offer a woman. Nothing has changed."

He moved, and she thought he was getting up. Instead, he shifted his weight off her, then rested his head beside hers. His hand lay possessively on her midriff. She let herself relax against him. "Why didn't you tell me that the first time we made love, instead of leaving like you did?"

Deke hesitated, not sure if he should admit the truth. But she deserved his honesty. "Because you tempt me to stay more than any other woman ever has. And I can't. Don't depend on me, Mary Beth. I'm not made that way."

"Because of the rodeo?" His whole body stiffened, and for a moment she wished the words back.

He eased away from her. "It's more than that," he said.

An uncomfortable silence fell between them. His tone held a harsh edge. Instinct told Mary Beth that the change had nothing to do with her. "Winning is that important? Or is it the thrill, the rush?" She'd heard that cowboys get rodeoing in their blood, that it became their life.

A muscle in his jaw ticked. "It's complicated."

Mary Beth ran her hand across his shoulder. She loved the freedom of touching him, loved the feel of his skin beneath her palm. "Then explain it to me, Deke." He took so long to reply that she didn't think he was going to. When he did, an underlying sadness lingered in his voice.

"My father and I enjoyed the rodeo. We used to go together and watch. When I was old enough, even though my mother was dead set against it, Dad let me train and then compete." Looking away, he swallowed hard, re-membering the stricken look on his father's face, the pain he'd caused the man he'd idolized. "I miss him."

Though she vaguely remembered Jacob McCall, Mary Beth recalled that he was well liked. She sensed that Deke and his father had been close. Did his drive to compete have something to do with their relationship? Or was Deke, in some confusing way, trying to restore memories of his father through the rodeo? Whatever the reason, he still hadn't accepted the loss of his father.

Have you?

Mary Beth closed her eyes. How could she accept her own loss when her father never cared? Dammit, she didn't want to think of him on her birthday, not when she was happy. She didn't want to feel the pain, the hurt. But how could she help Deke with his distress when she couldn't even deal with her own?

Opening her eyes, she found Deke watching her. "It hurts losing someone you love," she said softly, thinking of her mother. Time had eased the pain, but hardly a day went by that Mary Beth didn't think of Della.

Deke's eyes darkened. "On my father's grave, I made a promise to him that I'd win the title for him."

She turned toward him more and propped her head on her arm so she could see his face. "You were young, Deke."

He stared solemnly back at her, his jaw taut. "I was old enough to know what I was doing. Old enough to take responsibility for my actions. I said some terrible things to my father."

Puzzled by his answer, she frowned. "I'm sure your father loved you," she said gently.

He brushed her hand from his arm, then rolled away

from her and sat on the edge of the bed. "We had a terrible argument the night before he was in that airplane crash."

Mary Beth remembered that day, remembered hearing that his parents had been killed. She'd felt terribly for them all. They'd seemed the perfect family, then suddenly, tragically, their lives were forever changed. "What happened?"

Deke gave a bitter laugh as he looked at her over his shoulder. "I'd been pushing his buttons for days. That night I sneaked out of the house. He embarrassed me in front of my friend by coming after me and hauling my butt home. I was so angry at him."

Ashamed, Deke had never shared what happened with anyone, not even with his siblings. But something deep inside him drove him on. "I told him I hated him." He paused and drew in a breath. "I didn't know he would die the next day," he confessed, his voice ragged. He forced himself to look at Mary Beth, expecting to see disgust in her eyes. He was shaken when he discovered compassion and concern.

Mary Beth sat up and drew her knees to her chest. Her eyes filled with tears. Two years ago she'd thought Deke callous and self-serving. She had let that view of him fester, allowing herself to erect a barrier against his charm. It was unsettling to discover that she'd been so wrong about him. The demon driving Deke to pursue a bull-riding title was the fact that he'd let his father down—and himself, as well.

Her gaze slowly drifted over him. Unapproachable, he sat with his back to her, his muscles stiff and unyielding, his shoulders tense. He was hurting, and her heart ached for him. She wanted so much to ease his pain. "Your father was a good man, Deke. He loved you. I'm sure he knew you didn't mean what you said. You can't go on torturing yourself forever.''

She'd barely finished speaking when he stood and snatched his pants from the floor. ''I didn't ask for your opinion.'' He pulled his jeans on with jerky movements.

His words cut into her, for a moment stealing her breath. ''I'm sorry,'' she said automatically. But Mary Beth sensed that his sudden emotional withdrawal stemmed from unsettled issues with his father, rather than his feelings for her.

Still, it hurt when he pulled away. He'd been too busy running from his ghosts to deal with his past. Of all people, she understood. Her issues with her own father were why she'd remained in Crockett, why she continued to give every waking breath to making Paradise a success.

So the decision was hers. Protecting her heart from further pain, she could accept what he offered of himself, knowing he would never be there for her. Or she could say goodbye to him now and watch him walk out of her life.

Again.

Deke turned toward her, his expression remorseful. ''Look, I didn't mean—''

''It's okay,'' she said, interrupting him. She got out of the bed and scooped up her clothes. Her hands trembling, she slid on her panties and jeans, then turned away to put on her bra.

He cursed under his breath. ''I just wanted you to understand that I can't stay.''

Glancing over her shoulder, she struggled to keep her face impassive when emotions inside her were exploding. Whether or not being with him led to something deeper, she wasn't ready to let Deke walk out of her life. ''I'm not expecting anything from you. I told you that,'' she answered very softly.

She fumbled with her shirt for a minute before she was able to get it on. ''You're reading way too much into this.'' She said the words she knew he wanted to hear. ''Making love with you was special, but you don't have to worry. I'm not going to fall in love with you.''

Wishing he could see her face, Deke narrowed his gaze on her. ''What?''

She turned and faced him, her heart pounding. ''Regardless of what you think, I'm not waiting around for a man to make my life complete.'' She'd given that dream up long ago. ''Nor am I staying in Crockett.''

Deke felt gut punched, which was ridiculous. He didn't *want* her to fall in love with him, did he? And he *wasn't* in love with her. No chance of it. Hell, he'd even spelled it out for her.

So why did it bother him that she had dismissed their intimacy as little more than enjoying an afternoon of heat between the sheets? ''What are you talking about?'' His tone sharpened. ''Where are you going?''

''I'm leaving Crockett as soon as I get Paradise solvent. I enjoyed living in San Antonio, a lot more than here. Besides, there are a lot of places I've never been. I'm not sure where I'll end up living.''

That explained all those travel magazines he'd seen around her house. He sensed that she wasn't telling him something. ''If you miss it so much, what's holding you here?'' She didn't seem in any big hurry to head back to San Antonio. Nor did she appear to have the money to travel the world like a socialite.

She shrugged. ''Like you, I have something to prove. My father spent his entire life letting me know what a disappointment I was to him.'' She walked to her dresser and picked up her brush. "I was the daughter he never wanted," she told him, dragging the brush through her hair.

That explained a lot, Deke decided. Though she acted as if she hadn't been hurt by her father, he could see in her eyes that she was still suffering. Why else hadn't she cleaned out his things? Apparently, the pain of losing him was still too fresh to sort through years of memories. "And it means that much for you to make the ranch a success?" he prompted, wanting to know what she was thinking. "Your father isn't here, Mary Beth. He won't even know whether or not you succeed."

"Your father isn't here, either," she said pointedly. "Besides, I'm doing this for me." His expression said, "yeah, right," and she glared at him. "*I am.* For years I begged him to let me help around the ranch, but he totally ignored me because I was a female. Now I'm the one in charge, the one making the decisions." She tossed the brush on her dresser. "I *am* going to make this ranch a success. I know I can do it. Especially now that I have Lightning and Lady." Thinking of the money she needed to hold on to the ranch, she sent up a silent prayer that she would succeed. She couldn't bear the thought of failing, especially in front of Deke.

Her gaze drifted lazily over him. Just looking at him made every breath she took just a little bit more exciting. Having him in her bed, well, that was a dream come true. Whatever the cost to her heart, at the moment she just couldn't pass up the chance to be with him.

You can do this. You've been crazy about him all your life. You can enjoy being with him, making love with him, and when it's over, you'll survive.

She shook her head to clear her mind, then said,

"Speaking of the dogs, I wonder what they've been up to."

Deke went to the door and opened it. Just as he'd suspected, Lightning and Lady were waiting for them. They jumped up in unison and shuffled with excitement. "Hey, guys!" His greeting was met with more prancing, then the dogs ran over to Mary Beth. Deke followed them and stood beside her. "If you want, we can go outside and work them a little before I leave."

Her stomach in knots, Mary Beth gave both dogs a pat. "I need to freshen up a bit. Why don't you go on out, and I'll join you in a few minutes?"

Deke looked at her flushed skin and swallowed hard. All he really wanted to do was to drag her back into bed and make love to her, but that wasn't an option. He needed to get on the road soon, needed to get his mind on the next competition.

Struggling between his promise and his desire for Mary Beth, he said, "All right. I'll go on out and get things ready." But he didn't walk away. Instead, he leaned down and kissed her. Her lips were soft and pliable, and the way they clung to his made him groan. He forced himself to pull away. Without looking back, he left the room, the dogs in tow.

Mary Beth sucked in a deep breath. Oh, she was in trouble. She'd thought she could control her feelings for Deke, but after he'd revealed the turmoil of his past, she wasn't so sure. Shaking, she hurried to finish dressing.

By the time she got outside, Deke had saddled two horses. They spent the next couple of hours working some of her cattle with the dogs. Mary Beth tried to focus her energy on learning about the dogs' herding ability and not think about her ever-changing emotions about Deke. As she watched the border collies work, she was amazed by their skill all over again.

Afternoon approached, and the time for Deke to leave drew near. After spending the morning in each other's arms, she'd feared that things would be awkward between them. She couldn't have been more wrong. He'd seemed perfectly at ease with her, and she'd enjoyed being with him. Too much. She'd treasured every moment. When it came time for Deke to leave, he pulled her into his arms and kissed her thoroughly. As she watched him drive away, tears gathered in her eyes, and her heart ached. He'd said he'd be back.

She wanted to believe that he would.

Hot and sweaty, Mary Beth bedded down the horses for the night, then dragged herself into the house. She ached all over.

Entering the kitchen, she drank two full glasses of water, then summoned enough energy to feed Lightning and Lady. She thought fleetingly about finding something to eat for herself, but in the end was just too tired to put forth the effort. Right now she needed a hot bath. And rest. Lots of rest.

She went straight to the bathroom and filled her bathtub with water as hot as she could stand it. Her muscles were hurting so much it was all she could do to strip off her clothes. Literally crying out from the torture of raising her leg to get into the tub, she sank her aching body into the steamy water.

It had been a rough two days. With a bit of trepidation and a lot of reservation, she'd begun the process of seeding hay for the next year. Why she bothered was anyone's guess. She hadn't had a good crop this year. And she didn't even know if she'd be here in the spring. Still, she figured it wouldn't hurt to try another crop.

She'd spent the entire first day out in the field. The weather had started to change, and autumn had officially arrived. That night she hadn't been too sore, so she'd tackled the second day of seeding with even more vigor. That had been a vital mistake. Now she was exhausted.

The reality was that, as she'd suspected, no one had answered her advertisement for help. It was time for calving, and she wasn't going to be able to handle that alone. She needed to separate the spring calves from their mothers.

She'd toyed with the idea of calling Jake McCall and asking for help. In the end she decided against it. She felt awkward asking him for help since she'd slept with Deke.

As she crawled into bed, Lightning and Lady wandered into the room. She gave both dogs a pat, praised them for their hard work during the day, then watched them settle on the floor. Every time she looked at them she thought of Deke, and every time she thought of Deke she longed to see him.

Where was he tonight, she wondered. Was he alone? Was he thinking of her?

Lightning and Lady began barking just as Mary Beth finished eating the last bite of her toast. Seconds later she heard the roar of a motor and was amazed at the dogs' keen sense of hearing. Then her heart thumped. No, it couldn't be Deke! Still, she jumped up from her chair, raced to the window and peered out.

"Of course it isn't Deke," she told herself as she watched a white pickup truck pull into the yard and stop in front of her house. "You're wasting your time thinking

about him. He's in Lubbock, and he probably isn't thinking of you.''

She recognized Matthew McCall as soon as he got out
of the truck. Glad to see him, she walked outside to greet
him, stopping on the porch as he approached. Each time
she saw the youngest McCall male, she was struck by his
resemblance to his father, from his chiseled face and sturdy
built body, right down to the swagger of his walk. He'd
filled out since he'd come to Texas to live and had grown
at least five inches. He gave her an easy smile as he approached, and Mary Beth suspected that he must be driving
the girls of Crockett absolutely crazy.

''Hello, Matthew.'' She hadn't seen him in a while, but
she wasn't exactly surprised by his visit. He'd stopped by
occasionally, usually arriving by horseback because he'd
been working nearby.

''Hi.'' Matthew barely had time to speak before Lightning and Lady were vying for his attention. ''Hey, who
are these two?'' He bent down to give both dogs his
attention.

''Lightning and Lady. I just got them a few days ago,''
she said, but she didn't reveal they were a gift from Deke.
She doubted that he'd told his family he'd been with her.

''They're something.''

''They've been a great help.'' Glancing at the truck, she
said, ''Driving now, huh?''

Matthew glanced at the shiny truck, then back to Mary
Beth. ''It's not mine. Dad's letting me drive it some,
though. I can only go on the back roads by myself.'' He
shrugged. ''I don't have my license, yet.''

''I see.'' Smiling, she leaned against the porch railing.
It was nice to have someone to talk to. Better still to have
a reason to put off starting her work. ''How is everyone

at the Bar M? I saw Ashley in town recently with the girls. They're growing like weeds.''

Looking up at her, Matthew put a foot on the lowest step and leaned his arm on the railing. He adjusted his ball cap up slightly. "They sure are. Taylor is, too.''

"I bet they keep everyone busy.''

"Yeah, they do,'' Matthew readily agreed with a laugh. "Russ and Lynn had a baby boy last month. They named him Shayne.''

"I'd heard they had a boy.''

"He's real cute. Actually, it's great having cousins. They're all a lot of fun.''

"How are things at the Bar M?''

"Good. We've just finished seeding.''

Mary Beth tamped down the envious feelings inside her. The Bar M had the equipment and manpower to get the job done in the minimum amount of time. "I've planted, but my crops haven't done well the past two years. I'm hoping to start separating calves from their mothers to-day.'' It would be a daunting job that would take days.

Matthew straightened. "I heard you needed some help. Have you hired anyone yet?''

"No, I haven't. Why? Have you heard of someone wanting work?'' she asked, and hope began to build inside her. "I'd be willing to take anyone, as long as he's not an ax murderer.''

Matt chuckled. "Well, I'm not an ax murderer.''

She stared at him, her mouth dropping open. "You? Why on earth would you want to work for me? Your father owns one of the most profitable ranches in the county. I'm sure there's plenty of work on the Bar M.''

"I'd be grateful if you gave me a chance. I'll work real hard for you.''

She came down two steps toward him. "I know you

would, Matthew. That's not in question. But why would you want to?'' Mary Beth fleetingly wondered if Deke had something to do with Matthew coming over to ask for work. Had he gone home and told his family about the horrendous condition of her ranch?

"I'm trying to earn some money for my own truck,'' Matt explained. "Dad said he'd help me get one, but only if I came up with part of the money.''

His explanation put her at ease. Embarrassed to admit how bad things were for her, she told him, "I can't pay that much.''

"I'm willing to work for minimum wage,'' Matthew said.

Her eyes widened. "Really? Are you sure? What does your father say about this? Like I said, there must be plenty to do at the Bar M.'' Afraid he'd have second thoughts, she tried to hold back her excitement.

"It was his idea for me to come over. He saw your ad in the paper and thought it would be a good experience for me to work for someone else. All I have to do is keep up with my chores. So, how about it?''

Mary Beth couldn't have asked for anyone better to come along. Though she'd put an ad in the paper, she'd been a little nervous about hiring a stranger. But she liked Matthew, and she could trust him. "You're hired. When do you want to start?''

"How about now?''

With a relieved smile, she shook his hand. "You've got a deal.''

With the help of Lightning and Lady, they spent the remainder of the day separating calves. Spotting cows ready to give birth, they moved them to a pasture closer to the house. Mary Beth enjoyed working with Matthew, but she hadn't been prepared for his fascination of his un-

cle's exploits at the rodeo. He talked incessantly about
Deke's competing. While she tried her best to listen with
indifference, Mary Beth shamefully hung on every word.

But when Matthew began talking about the women who
hung around the rodeo, she had a hard time concentrating
on work. According to Matthew, who obviously admired
his uncle's prowess with women, there were plenty of
ladies at the rodeo flirting with Deke, willing to keep him
company.

Her heart dropped. Well, what had she expected?
They'd shared a mutual attraction, not an exclusive relationship. She clamped her teeth together. It hurt thinking
about him with other women.

Lord, she was a fool. Deke wasn't sitting in some hotel
room pining for her, was he? No, he was out enjoying
himself. And she was wasting precious time and energy
thinking about him.

Still, she couldn't seem to stop.

As she watched Matthew drive away late in the afternoon, Mary Beth heard the phone ring. The sun had already begun to set, and she suspected that it was Catherine,
Matthew's mother, wondering if her son was on his way
home.

But it wasn't Catherine's voice she heard when she answered the phone. Instead, Deke greeted her with his usual
teasing manner.

"Hey, sweetheart. Missing me?"

Mary Beth didn't answer. She couldn't. Her entire body
had gone still.

Get a grip!

"Hello?"

"I'm here, Deke," she said, straining to keep her tone
even and not let him know how thrilled she was just to
hear his voice. "How are you?"

"Tired. I've been competing for the past few nights. By the time I get in, it's late. I wasn't sure when to call because I didn't want to wake you."

"I'm usually in bed early," she agreed, trying not to react to the warmth of his tone.

"How are you?"

Mary Beth sat in a kitchen chair and propped her feet on another, knees bent. "I'm doing okay." Well, she was, except that her heart was beating a mile a minute. "Did you know that Matthew is working for me a few hours each day?"

"Yeah, I talked to Jake a few minutes ago. How's Matt doing?"

"It's wonderful having him here. He's been a lot of help. We started bringing in the calves."

"Sounds like a busy day."

Gnawing on her lip, Mary Beth hesitated, then said, "I'd better let you go. I'm sure you're tired. I know I am." She thought it best to keep their conversation short. Otherwise she was going to blurt how much she missed him.

"Okay, I'll let you go, then."

She whispered goodbye, then hung up the phone, feeling ridiculously weepy. Hearing Deke's voice had been torment. She *had* to stop thinking about him every waking moment. She couldn't give him the power to break her heart.

Over the next couple of weeks Matt helped her finish separating the spring calves from their mothers. Together they managed to get them weighed. Mary Beth didn't know what she would have done without him or his company.

Deke called a few times, but she kept to her decision and talked with him briefly. She wasn't going to pine away for him. She already cared about him too much as it was. This time when he left, he'd break what was left of her heart.

As if her heart was her biggest problem at this point. The ranch was in deeper trouble than she'd thought. Though she'd sold the largest part of her herd, she was still a thousand dollars short of paying the mortgage.

She had no idea how in the world she was going to come up with the money. She rubbed her temple as her head began to throb. If she didn't scrape up that last thousand, she was going to lose the ranch.

Mary Beth dropped her head in her hands. What was she going to do now?

Eight

Deke didn't know what in the world was wrong with Mary Beth, but he was determined to find out. He took the turn to Paradise a little faster than the narrow road allowed. The truck kicked up gravel and clouds of dust, then he brought it back under tight control.

For the past couple of weeks he'd had a hard time concentrating on bull riding. Hell, last night he'd earned his lowest score ever! He had Mary Beth to thank for that. Thinking about her consumed all of his thoughts. He missed her. And he worried about her, dammit!

Though Matt was working a few hours a day, the rest of the time Mary Beth was alone to handle everything else on her own. There was plenty of hard, dirty work on a ranch—more than any woman should have to handle alone.

Deke thrummed his fingers on the steering wheel as he tried to analyze his feelings for her. From the first time they'd made love, he'd known she was a threat to his heart in a way no other woman had been. Even now, when his mind should be on the rodeo, all he could think about was her.

When you're on the back of a raging bull, the last thing you should be thinking about is a knockout redhead with a smart mouth and a sassy attitude.

It was a miracle that he hadn't been killed.

Maybe he would have had better luck competing if Mary Beth had paid him a little attention when he called her. It would've set his mind at ease to know that she'd been thinking about him, too.

Did she think about him at all? Did she lie awake at night and wish he was there with her, making love to her?

Hell if he knew. He'd made a special effort to stay in touch with her, wanting to hear her voice. But she'd kept their conversations brief and impersonal. She'd always seemed in a hurry to end his call, like she didn't have time for him.

Well, he'd had enough. If she didn't want to hear from him, all she had to do was say so. He could take it.

Yeah, right. So why are you making a pit stop at her house?

Deke shook his head. He'd talked with Matt several times since his nephew started working for her. At first he'd been relieved that Matt was there watching out for her part of the time. But almost right away Deke had noticed that her attitude toward him had changed. Maybe she was embarrassed to let his nephew know about their relationship.

Relationship. Is that what they had? What did you call it when a woman stole your sanity? When you closed your eyes at night and dreamed of a green-eyed beauty that you couldn't seem to forget? When you wanted that woman so badly you ached with it?

Deke pulled into the yard and skidded to a halt in front of Mary Beth's house. With dust clouding around him, he jumped out, slammed the door and pocketed his keys. He rounded the truck, and Lightning and Lady raced up to him, tails wagging.

"Hey there you two." They pranced around his legs, but he only glanced at them with a frustrated look. "Stay out here, guys. This may not be pretty."

Deke tried to think rationally as he stalked toward the house. "Okay, calm down," he ordered himself. "You're not going to get any points by running roughshod over her. You know how stubborn she is."

Great! Now you're talking to yourself!

He took his Stetson off and slapped it against his thigh. Taking a couple of deep breaths, he rapped his fist on her door. A few seconds later it slowly opened. Deke stared at the woman who'd been driving him crazy for the past two weeks.

His gaze drifted over the swell of her breasts beneath her soft white tank top, then lower over those long, slim legs encased in snug jeans. Blood pumped furiously through his heart at the sight of her.

"Hello, sweetheart," he said easily, ignoring the adrenaline rush that demanded he haul her against him and seal her mouth with his.

"Deke!" Mary Beth's eyes widened, then she blinked. "What are you doing here?" Taken aback, she stood frozen in place. She flicked her gaze over the length of him. His navy-blue shirt was tucked neatly into his blue jeans. Her heart tripped over itself.

Deke grinned. He'd caught her off guard. Good. That's the way he wanted her. Now they were even. "Came by to see my best girl," he said as he studied her. Her hair cascaded around her face and fell to her shoulders in soft waves. His gaze slid lower, appreciating every luscious curve before returning to her face.

Caution flickered in her eyes before she concealed it. *Best* girl. She wondered how many that included. "I thought you were in Tulsa." At least, that's where Matt had said his uncle would be.

He shrugged one big shoulder. "I needed something from home, so I took a slight detour." Though it wasn't true, his excuse sounded plausible. He'd come home for one reason only. He'd wanted to see her, hold her, touch her. Tilting his head, he gave her an engaging grin. "Well, are you gonna invite me in?"

"What? Oh, sure." A blush touched her cheeks as she stepped aside for him to enter. After he walked past, she closed the door and turned toward him.

Deke reached out to touch her, but she skirted around him. "I was about to make something for dinner," she said in a breathless rush as she headed for the kitchen.

Frowning, he followed her, the swaying of her hips messing with his libido. Her reaction to him confirmed his suspicions. Something was going on. He grabbed her arm and brought her around to face him. "What's wrong?"

Eyes remote, she jerked her arm free and stepped away. "Nothing."

"You don't seem all that thrilled to see me." She continued to avoid his gaze, building his frustration. He'd come a long way to see her. The least she could do was seem appreciative.

She tossed her head, then leaned back against the doorjamb. "I don't know what you mean. I'm glad you took the time to stop by." Her breathing accelerated as if in direct contrast with her words. "Have you been to the Bar M yet?"

"No," he admitted, an edge to his voice. "I drove straight here."

Though surprised, Mary Beth didn't blink. As casually as she could manage it, she walked across the room. "Oh. Well, are you hungry? I could make you something to eat." She gripped the handle of the refrigerator door, then turned back to look at him. Her gaze landed on his face.

"I'm hungry, all right." The softness of his voice was in direct contrast to his heated gaze. He stalked over to her. "But not for food." Her unique scent drifted to him, and his nostrils flared.

Mary Beth squared her shoulders. "That's all I'm offering." She didn't have to explain what she meant. Deke's thunderous expression told her he understood. She had to stop herself from wincing.

"What's wrong?" he demanded, losing control of his temper. He tossed his hat into a chair.

"Nothing." She shrugged indifferently, though her nerves were stretched to capacity.

Deke jammed his hands in the pockets of his jeans to keep from dragging her against him. He rolled his shoulders, but it did little to ease the tension building inside him. He hadn't expected her to throw herself at him, but neither had he expected to slam into the invisible wall she'd put up between them. Something was seriously wrong, and he didn't have a clue as to what it was. Unless…

She's seeing someone else.

He hissed out a breath.

"Who is it?" he half growled.

Confused, Mary Beth searched his face. "What?"

Seething, Deke raked her with his eyes as he moved

closer, crowding her space. "Who are you seeing?" The thought of her with another man nearly drove him insane. He pressed his lips together to keep from saying something he'd regret.

A calmness stole over Mary Beth. She stiffened her spine, then very deliberately raised her hands and shoved him away from her. Her hands on her hips, she narrowed her gaze on him. "You've got some nerve, Deke," she said very calmly.

"Me?" he countered hotly. "I came all this way to see you, and you act like you can't even give me the time of day." He glowered at her as she moved farther away from him.

She laughed bitterly, then covered her mouth with her hand. The irony of his accusing her of being with someone else was the last straw. "Oh, I see. You think because we slept together, that gives you the right to say who I can or can't see? From what I've heard, you haven't exactly been celibate while you've been away." She jutted her chin at him. "What gives you the right to make demands on me?"

Speechless, Deke stared at her, his mind whirling. What was she talking about? Since he'd been away, Mary Beth was all he could think about. Walking over to her, he arched one blond brow. "I don't know who you've been talking to, but—"

"Oh, Matthew's been very forthcoming with your exploits at the rodeos—and I don't mean bull riding."

She was serious! Deke almost laughed, but caught himself. The thought of being intimate with anyone other than Mary Beth was crazy. "Matt? What the heck would he know?"

"Oh, please. He's told me all about the women who hang around the rodeo just waiting for a chance to jump in your bed."

Understanding dawned on Deke. *She was jealous!* "Is that what all of your frostiness on the phone was about?" he asked, then gave her a cocky grin.

"I was *not* being frosty."

"Oh, yes, you were."

"No, I wasn't," she snapped. Marching up to him, she poked her finger at his chest. "And don't you dare act as if you don't know what I'm talking about." His grin grew a little wider, and her temper went up a notch. "It's not funny, Deke. You can't just drop in here anytime you want convenient sex!"

"Convenient sex? Sweetheart, driving for hours on the road to see you after three full days of competing is anything *but* convenient." Deke's eyes twinkled with amusement. "I'll admit that there are women who hang around every rodeo like groupies." She opened her mouth to speak, but he gently touched his finger to her lips. "But I swear, I haven't been with another woman since I left you."

She blinked, stunned by his declaration. "Really?" Her heartbeat grew erratic.

"Really." He laid a hand on her shoulder, then drew her toward him. Cupping her chin, he lifted her face until their gazes met and locked. "The only woman I want to be with is you," he said huskily.

"Deke—"

His mouth swooped down on hers, stealing her words, her breath. Mary Beth's eyelids drifted shut as she gave herself to his kiss. For a moment everything inside her went hazy. Clutching his shirt, she leaned into him, savoring the feel of his mouth on hers, his taste, the very essence of him.

He backed her against the refrigerator, molding himself to her, rock-hard muscle against her soft, feminine curves.

His warmth seeped into her, and she opened her mouth, deepening the kiss.

Hot, urgent need raced through her, turning her legs to jelly. The caress of his tongue drew a pleading groan from deep within her. She dragged her mouth from his. "Deke, oh, please," she rasped, moving her hips against him.

"Hold on, sweetheart," Deke whispered, his lips brushing her ear. "I didn't come all this way for a quick tumble. I want all of you, everything you have to give." But even as he whispered the words, he was tugging her shirt up, baring her to him. Gratified she wasn't wearing a bra, he touched her erect nipple with his fingers.

A cry of pleasure escaped her lips. Already hard for her, Deke felt like he was going to burst right out of his jeans. Her hands cupped his face, and her lips found his again. Passion flared, clothes disappeared. Their boots hit the floor with soft thuds as they landed on the discarded mound of clothes.

"The bedroom," he muttered thickly, clad only in his jeans. Together they moved as one. He shoved her panties off, and they fell on the hallway floor. Their progress toward the bedroom momentarily forestalled, Mary Beth moaned as he lowered his mouth to her breasts. Cupping the generous mounds of flesh in his hands, he suckled one hard nipple.

Gasping for air, she strained toward him. The pleasure was so intense, so exquisite, that her body pleaded for release. Continuing to give his attention to her breasts, he slipped his arm around her back and draped her over it. As his lips and tongue savored her, he looked up. Her eyes were half-closed in ecstasy. He slowly slid his palm up her thigh, then between her legs. His finger slid into her.

Hot and moist, she tightened her legs around his hand.

Her eyes completely closed, and she gasped, then he felt her quiver as her hips began to move.

Mary Beth writhed in his arms. Deke lowered her to the floor, then worked his jeans off, grabbing a packet from his pocket before tossing them aside. He nudged her legs apart with his, then he sheathed himself and slipped inside her. His arousal felt hard and hot, filling her completely. Intense pleasure inside her began to build with a magnitude she'd never before experienced. She clung to him as his mouth ravaged hers.

Fire raged inside her as she locked her legs around his back. Her body out of control, she met him thrust for thrust. She felt him stiffen, and her muscles quivered around him, taking them both over the edge of sanity into another time, another place.

Deke lay there, his pulse beating so hard and fast that he was sure he was on the verge of a heart attack. He was convinced that he would never breathe normally again, wasn't sure he even cared if he did.

He stirred, then lifted his face to look at Mary Beth. Her cheeks were rosy, her skin warm. He brushed his lips softly against hers.

Mary Beth's lids lifted, and she looked at him. "We didn't make it to the bedroom."

Deke kissed her long and hard. "Ah, sweetheart, but I'm not nearly finished with you."

Desire lit a spark in her eyes. "Mmm, what else do you have planned?"

He stroked her breast, teased her nipple with his fingers. "A little of this." He moved his hips against hers. "A lot of this."

She slid her arms around his neck, touched a tender kiss to his mouth. "I'm ready when you are." Her hips moved against his. "Mmm, feels like you're about there."

Deke's eyes darkened as he watched her eyes glaze with passion. "Let's take this to the bedroom." This time he wanted her in bed, wanted to take it slow. He stood, then held out his hand to her. As she began to rise, he lifted her in his arms, carried her into her bedroom and laid her on the bed. He disappeared into the bathroom, then quickly returned to join her.

"How long can you stay?" she asked, already dreading the moment when he would leave.

Deke nibbled on her ear, then began planting kisses along her cheek. "I have to be in Tulsa by tomorrow evening." He caught her mouth in a searing kiss. When he lifted his lips, his eyes met hers. "And I have to get up early to get to the Bar M before I head out." Looking at her hair spread out on the pillow, Deke struggled to get his breath. "You're so beautiful," he whispered.

He cupped her luscious breasts in his hands. Her skin felt like silk beneath his fingers. His hand touched her nipple, gently twirled it with his fingers. She sighed, a soft, pleasurable sound that sent a surge of blood straight to his manhood. He rolled over and brought her body on top of his.

Mary Beth's stomach muscles tightened. Though she'd known that the rodeo came first, it still gave her a sense of loss when he spoke of leaving. "Then we'd better make the most of tonight," she whispered. Mary Beth scooted down his body, kissed his belly, then took him in her mouth. He groaned, a guttural sound that came from deep within him.

"Honey, I'm not gonna last another minute if you keep that up."

"Well, we don't want that, now do we?" She slid her body up his. Deke lifted her hips, then settled her on top of him. Mary Beth caught her breath at the intense pleasure of feeling him slide into her. "Oh, that feels so good."

Deke's hands molded her breasts as he began to move his hips. "I can make you feel a lot better." His eyes sought hers as he touched her nipples.

Mary Beth's head fell back. Sparkling, multicolored lights flashed before her eyes. She moved her hips in a rocking motion, meeting his thrusts, demanding more.

"Oh, my. Oh, Deke," she murmured, her voice husky, her breathing rapid. "Now."

Deke moved his hands slowly over her, burning every inch of her into his memory. He moved faster, deeper into her, then suddenly lost all sense of control as his body shattered into a million tiny pieces.

Mary Beth shifted to prop her head on Deke's chest. Her gaze moved over his face, studying the lines around his eyes, taking in his strong jawline, his sensual lips.

Her heart swelled.

She was hopelessly in love with him.

She sighed deeply. What was she going to do about it? What *could* she do about it?

Nothing. Don't do anything. Deke hasn't said a word about his feelings for you.

No, he hadn't. What he had done was make it perfectly clear that he had no room in his life for anything permanent with a woman. And that included her. So whatever he felt came a lot closer to desire. Possibly even genuine affection. But nothing deeper, nothing permanent.

Definitely not love.

Before she could further consider the reality of her feelings, he opened his eyes. His engaging grin endeared him to her all the more.

"Are you okay?" He held her tighter, absorbing her

warmth, and he lost the ability to think straight. His chest rose as he drew in a deep breath, struggling to get himself under control. He'd come there seeking answers. But he hadn't been ready to discover that his feelings for Mary Beth went a lot deeper than he was prepared for.

"Yes." She didn't give him a chance to read her thoughts. Instead, she slowly moved off him, then slid off the bed.

"Where are you going?" he asked, his eyes narrowing.

"To check on Lightning and Lady. They're still outside."

"They're dogs. They're supposed to be outside."

She turned her head, averting her gaze. "They're used to being inside with me. They probably think I've abandoned them."

Puzzled by her sudden withdrawal, Deke snatched her hand before she could move away. "Kiss me and I'll let you go." He linked her fingers with his.

Mary Beth arched her brow in amused disbelief. "Now, why don't I believe that?"

"I swear."

She gave in to her own desire for another taste of him. As their lips met, he slid his hand around her neck, pinning her lips against his. Mary Beth moaned into his mouth when his hand touched her breast.

She lifted her lips. "That's not playing fair," she complained, loving the way he made her feel. In answer, he cupped her thigh, ran his hand up her leg and squeezed her buttocks. "Deke."

"Hmm?"

"The sooner you let me go, the sooner we can make love again."

He set her free. "Well, if you insist…"

Mary Beth gave him a playful shove, and he fell back

onto the mattress. "I'm going to let the dogs in and feed them. Then I'll make us something to eat." Maybe by then she'd be able to think straight.

"I'm gonna grab a shower. Why don't you join me after you let the dogs in?"

Not bothering to dress, she walked to the door naked, then turned to look back at him. His hungry gaze made her tingle all over. "Maybe I will," she said, and gave him a sultry smile.

Deke couldn't get out of the bed fast enough.

Beneath the spray of warm water, they made love again. Then, after a long, intoxicating kiss, Mary Beth went to start dinner as Deke finished dressing. He pulled on his jeans, then sat on the edge of the bed as he slipped on his shirt. Picking up the telephone, he put in a call to the Bar M, letting them know where he was and to expect him in the morning. As he talked with Jake, Deke noticed a pad with some writing on it on Mary Beth's bedside table. Idle curiosity had him picking it up.

His gaze slid over the writing once, and he frowned. Studying it more closely, he realized he was reading notations Mary Beth had made concerning her mortgage. His lips twisted. She was a thousand dollars short.

Deke finished his call, then put the receiver in its cradle, his mind spinning. So he hadn't been wrong when he'd suspected that Mary Beth was in financial straits. He shook his head, then put the note back on the table. Frustrated, he stared at it. Why hadn't she confided in him? They were friends, weren't they? He wanted to help her. But how could he when she held her troubles inside?

Still thinking about her problem, he finished dressing, then went into the kitchen to join her. After they'd eaten, they laughed together as they gathered the clothes they'd tossed willy-nilly earlier. Exhausted, they climbed back into bed as the two dogs settled themselves on the floor. Deke wrapped his body around Mary Beth's and pulled her to him, the knowledge of her financial situation leaving him unsettled. She scooted her bottom closer and he nuzzled her neck, feeling more content than he had in years.

"Deke?"

"Hmm?"

"What time are you leaving?"

He closed his eyes and breathed in her scent. "I have to get an early start. I called the Bar M to let them know that I'd be by in the morning."

"Oh, I thought I heard you on the phone earlier," she said sleepily. "Did you tell them where you were?"

"Yeah. Why? Does it matter?" He opened one eye to gauge her reaction.

She gave a soft shrug. "I guess not," she answered, her voice quiet. Still, she wondered what his family thought when he mentioned he was at Paradise.

Deke closed his eye as he sensed her quiet withdrawal. He stroked her arm, then slid his hand up her midriff and found her breast. "Don't worry about it. My family really likes you. If anything, Ashley and Catherine are gonna have my hide for compromising you."

"Is that what you're doing?" She yawned. "I'm sorry I'm so tired, I think I could sleep a week."

Deke stroked her head with his hand. "Go to sleep sweetheart."

"I don't want to. I…want…to…"

Her words drifted off, and Deke smiled in the darkness. He'd worn her out. Well, he was pretty tired himself. He closed his eyes, but even as he drifted off, concerns about how Mary Beth was going to pay her mortgage haunted his mind.

* * *

Sometime during the night, Deke woke and they made love again. He knew he was playing with fire by staying with her, but he couldn't seem to resist the risk. She came into his arms half-asleep at first, and her eager response nearly shattered him. He brought her to climax with his hands and mouth, then buried himself deep inside of her. He drifted off to sleep, wondering how he was ever going to leave her in the morning.

When he woke, it was already going on seven. He opened his eyes and his gaze slid lazily over Mary Beth. She was still sleeping soundly in his arms. Resisting the urge to make love to her once more, he planted a soft kiss on her cheek. Thinking if he hurried he could see to some of her chores before he left, he eased himself out of the bed trying not to wake her.

A frown touched his brow. Why did it seem as if he was always leaving her? No matter how much he wanted to stay, he couldn't. He had to be in Tulsa this evening. He needed to broaden the gap between himself and his nearest competitor.

Moving quietly, he slipped on his clothes. As he bent over to grab his boots, he glanced at the notation Mary Beth had made about her mortgage. Damn! He really wanted to help her. She'd worked so hard trying to make a go of the ranch, only to come up short. If she didn't get that money, she'd lose everything.

Shaking his head, Deke stood and fished into his pants pocket for his wallet. He had the money Mary Beth needed with him. Opening his wallet, he counted out ten one-hundred-dollar bills, then tossed them on her dresser as he passed.

Knowing her stubborn pride, she'd probably have a fit

when she saw it, he thought with a chuckle as he quietly left the room, the dogs on his heels. Well, tough. If it bothered her that much, she could think of it as a loan.

Nine

By the time Mary Beth woke in the morning, Deke had already left. She looked at the indentation on the pillow next to her, and disappointment created a crater in her heart. Though she knew that he had to return to the rodeo, she wished he hadn't left without saying goodbye. It would have been wonderful to have awakened in his arms. Closing her eyes, she rested her hand against his pillow.

That's what you get for letting him near your heart.

Well, it wasn't as if she'd really had a choice. She'd been half in love with him most of her life. What started out as a crush had developed into much more over the years. Though she'd tried to keep her heart safe, she'd never really stood a chance at protecting it. Especially not since she'd moved back to Crockett. In San Antonio, Deke hadn't been around as a constant reminder of her feelings for him. She'd adjusted to living alone, believing she'd never see him again. Maybe if she'd stayed there, she would have eventually fallen in love with someone else.

Opening her eyes, she rolled over and stared absently at the ceiling. Her plans had taken an unexpected turn when she'd returned home to help her father. His subsequent death had changed the entire focus of her life. Even after she'd decided to stay at Paradise to try and make it a success, she hadn't had any real hope of a relationship with Deke. From what she'd heard, he was rarely home.

How was she to know that in the course of a few weeks, he would show up and turn her world upside down? Since spending time with him, she'd learned a lot about him— why he pushed himself so hard. His guilt over his relationship with his father drove him to try to make amends, to somehow find peace in his heart. She hoped he would one day be able to exorcize the memories that haunted him. He needed closure, needed to forgive himself.

While pondering Deke's strife, she gave some thought to her own role in their evolving relationship. Mary Beth understood him now. She felt that he cared for her, as much as he would allow himself. Haunted by regrets concerning his father, he'd closed himself off, refusing to let anyone near who would interfere with his goal of redeeming himself.

And that includes you.

Trust didn't come easy to her, but understanding his motives had caused her to let down her guard, to become vulnerable to him.

To fall hopelessly in love with him.

She sighed softly as she stretched her arms toward the headboard, then tucked her hands under her head. So she was in love with Deke. The realization didn't shock her as it might have a few weeks ago. Mainly because it didn't really alter her view of her life. She wasn't going to waste time dreaming that Deke would fall in love with her. For now she was content to have him be a part of her life.

Knowing she'd lost most of the morning, she figured she'd better get to her chores. She tossed off the sheet and put her legs over the side of the bed. As she got to her feet, she realized Lightning and Lady weren't in the room with her as usual. Deke must have fed them and put them outside so she could sleep. She smiled to herself. That was sweet of him. How long ago did he leave?

Her gaze went to the small alarm clock on the bedside table. Eight o'clock? Heavens, she couldn't remember the last time she'd slept so late. She smiled. Of course, she'd spent half the night making love with Deke.

She got up and went to her dresser in search of clean clothes. As she started to pull open a drawer, a flash of green caught her eye. What on earth…? A wad of bills lay beside her jewelry box, money that hadn't been there when she'd gone to bed.

Mary Beth stared at it. Where had it come…?

Deke?

He'd left her money? But why would he…?

Something painfully cold touched her heart as she stared blankly at the money. Then, her hand shaking, she slowly picked up the stack of bills. Her chest constricted, and she could hardly breathe.

He'd left her money!

Her stomach roiled. For a moment she thought she would be physically sick. She swallowed hard, forcing back the bile in her throat. She'd thought that Deke wouldn't hurt her, but she'd been so terribly wrong. Pain and humiliation engulfed her as her temper began to simmer. She didn't even stop to count the bills, didn't want to know what price Deke had put on having her.

Damn him! She'd believed him when he'd said he

wanted only her. But for a price? She hadn't realized that he meant as a…a mistress!

She fought against the tide of fury rising inside her. While she'd thought that they'd shared something so unbelievably special, Deke had only wanted sex. He'd cheapened the beautiful memory of passion they'd shared, made it sordid.

Tears sprang to her eyes. She crushed the wad of cash in her fist.

That low-down, yellow-bellied jerk!

How dare he?

How *dare* he!

Mary Beth jerked open her dresser drawer. She stuffed her legs into a pair of jeans so fast that she nearly tripped and fell. After yanking on her shirt and socks, she snatched her boots from the floor and tugged them on, then stomped from the room.

With the money still clutched in her fist, she stormed out the back door of the house. Besieged by Lightning and Lady, she ordered them in the truck. Eager for a ride, both dogs jumped into the cab without further prodding.

Seething, she turned the key in the ignition and the truck fired up. She gripped the steering wheel so tightly that her knuckles turned white. Muttering a curse, she mashed down the accelerator and the truck shot forward. Hoping the fresh air would clear her mind, she lowered the windows and let in the wind. It slapped her hair about her face. Unaware of anything except channeling her hurt, all she felt was blazing anger.

Mary Beth covered the distance between Paradise and the Bar M in ten minutes, less than half the usual time. Tearing into the yard, she jammed on the brakes. The small truck skidded to a halt at the McCalls' house, sending dirt and dust flying in clouds around it.

"Stay," she ordered the dogs. Her fist still wrapped around the money, she jumped out of the truck. Calling Deke every low-down name she could think of, she marched to the front door and gave it several sharp whacks. Only a moment passed before she pounded her fist against it again.

Ryder answered the door and frowned at her. "What the— Mary Beth! Well, hey, darlin'—"

"Where's that no-account brother of yours?" she demanded, not giving Ryder a chance to finish speaking.

Taken aback, Ryder eyed her with the caution due a mountain lion. Then he noticed the money fisted in her hand. "You must mean Deke."

"That's exactly who I mean," she said through clenched teeth. Her eyes scanned behind Ryder with fierce intent before slicing back to him. "Where is he?"

Ryder opened the screen door. He knew better than to interfere with a woman as angry as the redhead standing in front of him. "In the dining room," he told her. He pointed in that direction, then got the hell out of her way. She stormed past him. Ryder followed a safe distance behind her.

Mary Beth had been in the McCall house before and knew exactly where to go. When she burst into the dining room, she realized Deke wasn't alone. Her hot gaze swept past Jake, Catherine, Ashley and Matt before finally landing on her quarry.

Deke had been talking to Jake, but at Ashley's gasp, he'd looked up. Then he realized that Ryder had someone with him. His gaze moved to their guest, and his eyes widened. Mary Beth!

Grinning, he said, "Hey, sweetheart—" But his words faltered when he saw the look of white-hot anger on her face.

"Don't you 'sweetheart' me, you big, dumb jerk!" Mary Beth circled the room, aiming her finger at him. Her eyes blazing, she came to a halt in front of him. The confusion in his expression fueled the humiliation and outrage inside her.

Unmindful of their audience, she raised her fist and threw the wad of money at him. The bills fluttered in the air, then floated like feathers to the floor. "Just tell me one thing," she said, her voice lowering as she fought for control. "Do you pay every woman you sleep with?"

Startled, Deke's mouth fell open. "What? No, I—"

She jammed her hands on her hips. "Oh, so that makes me the first?" Fresh pain sliced through her heart.

"Wait, that's not what I—"

"I guess I played right into your hands, didn't I? I laid my heart right out there for you to stomp on. Well, let me tell you something, mister." She advanced on him, her face flaming with heat, her hands balled into fists. "You won't get another chance to hurt me, Deke McCall! I may have been stupid enough to believe your sweet lies in bed last night, but it won't happen again. Ever!"

Someone coughed, and Mary Beth gasped. She whirled around. Suddenly she became fully aware that she'd aired their intimacy with Deke's family staring at them. A mixture of shock and disbelief sent a rush of blood to her face. Her hand went to her mouth, muffling her cry of despair. She nearly fainted when she realized that Matthew had witnessed her entire tirade.

Tears exploded in her eyes. Mortified, sucking in a gulp of air, she stammered, "Oh...I'm so sorry. I—" The words caught in her throat. Her chest heaving, she rushed from the room. Someone touched her as she brushed past, but she didn't stop to see who it was. By the time she reached the door, she was running. Somehow Mary Beth made it safely to her truck. Tears streaked her cheeks as she started the engine, threw the truck into gear and stomped on the gas.

She never looked back.

Stunned, Deke tried to comprehend what had just happened. For a full ten seconds no one in the dining room said a word. When the brittle silence was finally broken, it was by Ryder. Tugging at his mustache, he sliced a hard look at his younger brother.

"Hell, Deke. Have you lost your mind? Paying Mary Beth for sex like she's some kind of—"

"Ryder!" Ashley blurted out, smacking him on the arm. She darted a look in Matt's direction.

"Maybe you'd better go outside, Matt," Catherine McCall said, and she gently touched her hand to her son's shoulder.

Matthew ignored his mother's suggestion. He glared at Deke, disapproval in his eyes. "I'm old enough to stay," he argued. His gaze narrowed on his uncle. "I can't believe you made Mary Beth cry like that, Uncle Deke," he charged. "She's a nice lady. And I think she really liked you. She talks about you a lot."

Deke's chair scraped the floor as he jumped to his feet. He glared back at Matthew, nearly wincing from his nephew's icy stare. "I didn't mean to hurt her," he stated, trying to keep his voice calm as he sorted through what had just happened. How had Mary Beth interpreted his trying to help her with the ranch into something as sordid as paying her for sex? His gaze swept past the displeased looks on his brothers' faces, then took in the disapproving glares of his two sisters-in-law. "I swear, I didn't."

Ashley walked over to him, her expression a mixture of

concern and confusion. "I certainly hope you have more of an explanation than that. The poor girl was in tears."

He put his hand out, palm first. "I need to talk to Mary Beth."

Jake moved away from the wall he'd been leaning on. "I think you owe us an explanation, as well." His tone held restrained patience. "Let's hear it."

Deke shook his head. "Later, I need to..." Aw, hell. He might stand a chance of making his family understand, but he wasn't so sure when it came to Mary Beth. His intentions had been honorable. He couldn't believe he had to explain his actions as if he were the devil incarnate. "Look, the truth is, I suspected that Mary Beth's been having financial trouble. I didn't want to embarrass her by asking straight out, so I hinted at it a few times. She's so damn prideful sometimes. And stubborn. She wouldn't even admit that anything was wrong."

Leaving the money on the floor, he began walking toward the door. "Last night I saw a note she'd made, indicating that she didn't have enough money to meet her mortgage payment. As I was leaving this morning, I remembered the note, then left the money so she'd be able to pay it." He gave a sardonic chuckle. "I never dreamed that she'd think I was paying her for—" He stopped speaking, looked at Matt and grimaced. "Well, you get the picture."

Matt stepped in front of him, impeding his progress. "Where are you going?"

Deke stiffened. "Not that it's any of your business, Matt, but I'm gonna try and set things straight." He started to moved around his nephew, but Matt stepped in front of him again.

"If your intentions aren't honorable, you ought to leave her alone."

Deke's tanned skin turned ruddy. He was proud of his nephew for standing up for Mary Beth, embarrassed that he was the one that Matt was trying to defend her against. "It's okay, Matt. I'm just going to talk to her and set things straight. That's all." He stepped around him, then left the room and went to his truck.

He glanced at his watch as he climbed inside and turned the engine over. At least he'd already packed for his trip. If he was going to make it to Tulsa on time, he'd have to leave straight from Mary Beth's. That was a big *if,* because he wasn't leaving until this misunderstanding between them had been sorted out. Though he'd seen her upset before, Deke had never witnessed anything like the temper she'd been in just now.

In hindsight, he thought, as he drove toward Paradise, he should have just come right out and asked Mary Beth if she needed a loan. But he'd only been trying to salvage her pride. And look what he got for trying! Mary Beth was furious, his family was upset with him, and for a minute there he'd thought Matt was going to clock him.

He hoped that by the time he arrived at Mary Beth's she'd cooled off. He wanted her to understand that he hadn't meant to insult her—that he'd only wanted to help her. How he could best accomplish that without hurting her further?

That damn ranch was falling down around her. She needed an investor, someone who... Deke smacked his hand against his forehead. That's it! He would offer to become an investor in her ranch—a silent partner. What she needed to make the ranch successful was capital. He'd give her the money she needed to continue running Paradise, plus she'd keep her pride.

Pleased he'd hit on the perfect solution, Deke relaxed a bit as he pulled up to Mary Beth's house. Lightning and

Lady barreled out of the barn as he got out of the truck. Knowing the dogs were never far from Mary Beth, he headed in that direction.

As he stepped inside the old structure, he saw her immediately. She glanced at him, and his chest constricted. Her eyes were swollen, her complexion scarlet. Regret slammed him. Though he'd thought he was doing something to help her, apparently he'd gone about it wrong. True to his nature, again he'd ended up hurting someone he cared about.

Ignoring him, she went about cleaning one of the stalls. He heaved a sigh and walked toward her, noticing the tightness in her carriage. She hadn't cooled off at all. It was going to take a lot of explaining to get that wounded look out of her eyes.

"Mary Beth, I want to talk to you."

"Well, I don't want to talk to you." She couldn't imagine what he could say that would explain his callous treatment of her.

"You have to give me a chance to explain."

She looked directly at him then, her expression tight. "I don't *have* to do anything I don't want to do."

Well, hell, that was clear enough. "You could at least listen to me. Don't I deserve that much?"

She threw down the rake and whirled toward him. If she didn't listen to him, he wouldn't leave, and at the moment she never wanted to see him again. That was the only way she'd stand a chance of getting past the pain and embarrassment he'd caused her. "Make it fast. I'm busy."

It wasn't much of an opening, but Deke seized it. "Look, sweetheart, I'm really sorry that you got the wrong idea when you saw that money. I didn't mean to hurt you." Her expression closed up, and frustrated, he blew out a breath. "Hell, Mary Beth, I can't believe you thought that I'd pay you for sex! I'd never do that!"

Glaring at him, she retorted, "What was I suppose to think when I saw that money lying on my dresser?"

"Well, I thought that you'd figure out I'd put it there so you'd have the money to pay your mortgage."

She blinked. "What?"

"Yesterday I saw the note you wrote to yourself about being short a thousand dollars on your mortgage. It was on your nightstand."

"You did?" She hadn't realized she'd left it there.

He shrugged and nodded. "I saw it when I used the phone. Look, sweetheart, I only wanted to help you. I'd sort of figured out that you were running short on money to keep the ranch going. When I was leaving this morning, I saw the note again. I left the money to help you, not to hurt you."

"If that's the truth, why didn't you just ask me about my finances?" she asked, not sure she believed him. His motives might have been magnanimous, but she realized that no matter how hard she tried to protect herself, he had the power to hurt her.

Somehow she'd lost control of her heart.

Deke grimaced. "Well, to tell you the truth, you were so determined to make the ranch profitable on your own, I was trying to spare your feelings." He walked toward her, closing the distance between them. He wanted more than anything to pull her against him, but he held himself back from touching her. "Things sort of blurred when we became lovers, Mary Beth. I care about you, and I didn't want to hurt you, so I didn't come right out and talk to you about what I suspected."

She rolled her eyes. Deke felt as if he was beating his head against a brick wall—a very prideful one. "I do care about you, honey.'' Damn, she was stubborn. ''To be totally honest, I'm a little hurt that you haven't talked to me about your financial situation,'' he admitted, his tone defensive.

Her eyes remained frosty. ''It's my problem, not yours.''

''That may be, but I want to help you.''

''Let me see if I can make this perfectly clear for you. You're the last man on earth that I want help from.''

He gave her a pleading look. ''Would you just hear me out? That's all I'm asking.''

Regarding him with wariness, she crossed her arms over her chest. ''All right. You've got exactly one minute.''

''I want to invest in Paradise. As a silent partner.''

Immediately suspicious, Mary Beth snorted. ''Now, why would you want to do that?'' Paradise was about to go under. Why would he want to risk money on it?

''It's the perfect solution for both of us. I have a lot of winnings saved up. I could put that money to good use on Paradise. Using it, you'd be able to get the ranch in the black. This is good land, and you've got a start on making the ranch a success. You just need capital.'' Shrugging indifferently, Mary Beth looked away from his watchful eyes. He'd thought she'd be happy about his offer. ''Are you willing to lose everything because of your pride?''

Her eyes sliced back to his. ''I'm not sure I care anymore.'' It was an honest answer. She was tired of fighting so hard to make the ranch a success. It was exhausting trying to do practically everything on her own. She was working herself to death. And for what? Nothing. Paradise was going under.

''I don't believe that.''

''It doesn't really matter to me what you believe. I wanted to make a go of it here, but it didn't work out.''

She'd learn to live with her failure eventually. "Maybe it's time I accepted the fact that my father was right about me. Maybe I can't run the ranch."

Deke swallowed hard. He didn't think she really believed that. But there was more at stake than just the ranch. He'd thought there was something between them. Had he been wrong? "And what about us, Mary Beth?"

"What about us? As you put it, we were lovers. That's all. I never expected it to last." It hurt to say the words, but after everything that had happened between them, she wasn't going to trust him again. Maybe she'd jumped to conclusions when she'd seen that money, but what was she to think? Deke could have asked her about the stability of the ranch, could have talked to her.

But he didn't. And apparently even he believed that she couldn't make a go of the ranch on her own. "I told you before that I wasn't staying in Crockett." She wondered now how she'd ever be able to stay without Deke's love. Sex would hold them together, but for how long? He'd said himself that he didn't have anything emotionally to give a woman...to give her. He'd made it clear that the rodeo was more important than anything or anyone.

In the end, he would walk away from her. Just like every other time.

Deke was a bit shaken by her casual dismissal of what they'd shared. Was that truly how she felt about him? He refused to believe that. And regardless, he wanted her at Paradise where he'd know she was okay. So he tried another tactic. "I'm giving you a chance to make this ranch successful. You've worked hard at it. Don't give up now. If you do, you'll regret it for the rest of your life."

If he could get her to agree to let him invest, that would keep her in Crockett. Right where he wanted her. "Think about it, Mary Beth. The reason it's been so tough for you is that your father left the place in shambles and strapped you with a load of debt. If you accept my offer, you can run this place any way you see fit. You call the shots. You make all the decisions. And the ranch will stay in your name.''

Mary Beth felt herself softening. He was offering her a chance to make Paradise the ranch she'd always believed it could be. She wanted so much to take a chance, but she just wasn't convinced she could trust herself around him.

When she remained silent, Deke looked at her, his gaze intense. ''Please believe me, sweetheart. I never meant to hurt you.''

Her eyes misted. ''I wish I could believe that, Deke.'' She wanted to trust him, but the only way she could was to keep him at arm's length. Every time she'd opened herself up to him, he'd managed to wound her in some way. Just like her father.

''Then take me up on my offer.''

She wanted to. Badly. He was offering her what she most wanted—to make Paradise a success. But at what price? Her heart? She just didn't know if it could take another beating. She had to protect herself some way. Somehow. Keeping their relationship platonic would save Paradise, and it would protect her heart. To Mary Beth, it was the only solution.

''If I say yes, then you have to agree to this being a business arrangement only.''

Uneasy, Deke shifted his stance. ''Meaning?''

''We'll keep things between us strictly business.'' Yes, she decided, that would work. She had a weakness where Deke McCall was concerned. And obviously, nothing permanent could come from a relationship with him. Maybe she'd survive if they kept things between them platonic.

Deke frowned. ''C'mon, Mary Beth—''

"I mean it."

He took in the stubborn tilt of her chin. Arguing with her wasn't going to get him anywhere. But if he agreed, she'd stay in Crockett. It was a small victory, but one he savored. Right now Mary Beth was still a little confused. He'd give her some time to come around. And if she didn't, well, he'd worry about that later. "If that's the way you want it, okay. I'll stop at the bank in town and set up an account for you to draw from."

"All right, then. Thank you."

Now that he had her acquiescence, Deke breathed a relieved sigh. It was far from over between them. Mary Beth just didn't know it yet.

Ten

As Deke drove up the road to Mary Beth's house, he spotted a pickup with two men heading toward him from the opposite direction. He touched the brim of his hat as the truck sped past, recognizing both Pete Newton and Charlie Baines. Both men gave a brief wave in his direction.

A few weeks had passed since he'd talked Mary Beth into letting him invest in Paradise. Deke surveyed her property as he neared the house. In that short time, she'd made a lot of improvements. She'd had the fencing surrounding her land completely replaced, the machine shed repaired and painted, and a new roof put on the barn. It seemed she'd had no trouble putting the men to work.

Pulling to a stop in front of her house, Deke switched the engine off, got out and stretched his legs. What was wrong with him? You'd think he could stay away from a woman who barely gave him the time of day. But no, here he was, wanting to see her so badly that he'd driven all night long to get there.

He'd called Mary Beth as often as he could from the rodeo. She'd always made a point to tell him how things were going at the ranch, letting him know each and every step she was taking to make it a success. As if he cared about the damn ranch!

Deke was back for one reason only. To see *her*. The finals would start in Vegas in three days. He was aware of his priorities, knew he had to give his full attention to bull riding. For the past few weeks he'd stayed away from Mary Beth and had done just that. He'd managed to hang on to the lead, but anything could happen in the finals. A couple of bad nights and he'd lose everything he'd worked for. His chance to win the championship for his father would disappear.

Deke had ridden the circuit for years, and each one had taken a toll on him. This year seemed to be his best chance to win the bull-riding title. He prayed it was. He just didn't think he had it in him to rodeo another year. His body ached all over. And he was getting damn tired of being thrown by raging bulls, icing down his aches and pains and traveling from city to city.

Recently Jake had asked him when he was going to settle down. Deke had sloughed off answering by cracking a joke. He'd never talked with his siblings about his reasons for continuing to participate in the risky sport of bull riding. It was easier to let his family believe that he loved the danger and thrived on the adrenaline rush than to admit to them that he told their father he'd hated him. Deke didn't think he could stand to see the disappointment in their eyes. There wasn't a day that went by that he wasn't haunted by their father's hurt expression.

Shaking off the unpleasant memory, he walked up the

steps to the porch and knocked on Mary Beth's door. His heart raced at the thought of seeing her.

Mary Beth was standing in the middle of her father's room surveying her day's work when she heard a knock at the front door. At the sound, Lightning and Lady jumped up and raced out of the room. She chuckled and followed them out, weaving around packed boxes stacked haphazardly on the floor.

It was rare for her to have visitors, and she welcomed the interruption. Going through her father's belongings had brought back all the feelings she'd thought she'd dealt with—his disappointment in her, her desire to please him, her resentment because he was never there for her and her mother.

And though she usually treasured her solitude, her life had been so empty without Deke. Was she ever going to get him out of her mind? Out of her heart?

A wistful sigh escaped her lips. She was no closer to forgetting him now than she'd been the day she'd told him she wanted to keep their arrangement strictly business.

Hah! That was a laugh. If he were here now, she would probably jump his bones!

She'd tried staying busy, focusing on work to keep him out of her mind. Since she'd hired two additional employees to work at the ranch, she'd had some free time to see to what needed to be done in the house. Starting in the kitchen, she'd worked her way through it, cleaning one room at a time, leaving her father's room until the very last.

She'd even tossed out all of the old travel magazines, thinking living in Crockett wasn't so bad. Now the inside of the house fairly sparkled—like it had when her mother was alive. For an old place, it didn't look half-bad.

The knock came again, louder this time. An edgy restlessness shifted through her as she neared the front door. Christmas was less than a month away, and she'd begun feeling the same gloomy, depressing emotions she experienced whenever she thought of the holiday.

For the past two years, she'd spent Christmas alone on the ranch. She'd pretty much ignored all the hoopla, preferring to treat it just like any other day. It had been for her. She'd had no loved ones to share the holiday season with.

Mary Beth thought of Deke and how nice it would be to spend the holidays with him. She loved him with all her heart. And time away from him had only made her miss him even more. Every time he called, every time she heard his sexy voice, her resolve to keep him at a distance melted another fraction. Since she hadn't made any progress toward forgetting him, she might as well have continued seeing him!

She muttered an oath beneath her breath. She had no one to thank but herself for being heartsick. It had been at her insistence that she and Deke share a business relationship. She couldn't fault *him*. Deke had respected her wishes.

Dammit! She should never have made that stupid stipulation. Maybe she would have ended up with a broken heart if she'd continued seeing him, but at least she would have enjoyed herself along the way!

Reaching the door, she opened it. Her breath caught. "Deke!" she squeaked. Her eyes widened as her gaze skimmed his body. His washed-out blue jeans hugged his hips and thighs, and his shirt brought out the blue in his eyes.

Deke felt her warm smile all the way to his toes. Damned if she didn't look happy to see him. Thrilled, he didn't question why. "Hey, sweetheart," he said, giving her an engaging grin. Hungry for the sight of her, his eyes lingered on her face. "Well, can I come in?"

"Oh…uh, of course," she stuttered. She nudged the dogs out of the way and moved aside for him to enter. Deke leaned down and patted Lightning and Lady as he came in, and Mary Beth blew out a breath as she watched his big hand lovingly stroke their fur.

He straightened, then put his arm around her and drew her to him. "I've missed you," he said thickly.

Startled, Mary Beth's eyes met his, and her heart tripled its beat. Her gaze slid to his mouth. All she could think about was how much she wanted his kiss. Maybe she was weak. Maybe she was just a fool, but at the moment, here in his arms, she wanted nothing more than to be with him. "I've missed you, too," she whispered, her voice raspy.

Deke aligned his body with hers. "Yeah?" He studied her, a bit surprised. What had happened to all her reservations? "How much?" he asked. Lowering his head, he briefly touched his lips to hers. She tasted sweet, like pure honey. He wondered if he'd ever get his fill of her.

She pressed her body closer, then smiled up at him. Her lips found his again, her teeth nipping his lower lip. "Mmm, so much."

Throwing caution to the wind, Deke kissed her deeply, hungrily. Blood roared in his ears. "Sweetheart, if this is how you're gonna welcome me, I'm coming home more often." His hands slid from her waist to her breasts, and when she eased away to give him better access, moaning that sweet, seductive sound she made when he found and touched her nipples, he gently rubbed his thumbs over each protruding bud.

Heat ignited in the core of her. Mary Beth's pulse began to race. His warm hands slid beneath her shirt, unclasped her bra, then he stripped them both off and tossed them to the floor. Desire burned in his eyes as they lowered to her breasts, to her dusky-pink nipples. His hands cupped her, testing their weight.

She gasped when he lowered his mouth and gently caught her taut nipple with his teeth. Oh, she'd missed this—the incredible way that this man could make her feel. She wanted to be loved by him, wanted to feel him inside her.

Her fingers found the buttons of his shirt and began slipping them through the buttonholes. Then she yanked the tail of it from his jeans and finished the rest. His shirt followed hers to the floor.

Her hands touched his skin, and Deke sucked in a breath. When she began to unbuckle his belt, he stopped her. "Sweetheart, I want you so much right now, if you touch me, I think I'll embarrass myself." With an expression of pure need, he scooped her up in his arms and carried her to her bedroom. "Let's do this right."

He eased her on the bed, and his lips sought hers hungrily. Slowly, methodically, he kissed a path down her throat to her breasts. His hand lifted one soft mound to his mouth, and he sucked her nipple, teasing it with soft bites. Mary Beth's eyes drifted shut as her hips began to move. Deke took her other nipple in his mouth as he stripped off her boots and jeans, then slid her panties down her thighs and tossed them aside.

His gaze swept over her. Something powerful moved inside him—a sensation unexpected and perplexing wrapped itself around his heart. And at that moment, Deke realized that he wanted Mary Beth for more than just this moment in time.

He slowly skimmed his hand down her body, loving the feel of her satiny skin beneath his palm. She lifted her eyelids and looked at him, her eyes glazed with passion. Deke's body trembled as she quivered beneath his touch.

His heartbeat quickened as he worked his clothes off. He joined her on the bed, aligning his body to hers. With each moment, each touch, he watched her, unable to get enough of looking at her.

Leaning down, he pressed his mouth to her neck. She smelled so incredible. Mary Beth turned her head toward him, seeking his mouth, his kiss. Her lips clung to his, hungry, yet gentle—urgent, yet so unbelievably soothing. He took his time with her, using his lips and tongue, tasting her skin as he trailed hot, wet kisses down her neck to the sensitive area between her breasts.

Mary Beth twined her arms around his neck, and she drew her to him. Deke's chest constricted as he positioned himself and joined their bodies. Fire raged inside him, and he sank all the way into her.

Perfect. She fit him so completely.

And when she moved against him, a storm of emotions came at him all at once. He trembled with the force of them, with his need for her. If he could make love to her for the rest of his life, it would never be enough.

But the fire she'd started inside him became a flaming inferno, raging through his body, stealing his ability to control his emotions. When she peaked, softly calling his name on her lips, he found his own release. He held her tightly to him as a million brilliant lights exploded like fireworks in his mind.

It was at that moment that Deke knew he was in love with Mary Beth.

"I woke up and you were gone." Deke gazed at Mary Beth as she stood at her father's dresser. His chest constricted. How could he leave her now? But he knew he couldn't stay. He wasn't good at relationships. He'd blown it with his father, hadn't he? What made him think that he wouldn't screw this up, too? When he'd decided to come and see her, he'd known that he couldn't stay long. Nothing had changed.

And he had no right to tell her that he loved her. Not yet. Not until after the finals. Even then, he wasn't sure it was a good idea. And if he didn't win…he wouldn't even let himself think about it.

Standing in her father's room, Mary Beth turned to look at Deke as he walked up behind her. He slipped his arms around her waist and brought her fully against him.

"I couldn't sleep," she said, and she closed her eyes for a moment, savoring the pleasure of being held in his arms. "I thought maybe I could get a few more things done in here." She turned in his arms and pressed herself to him, the warmth in his eyes touching her heart. "Do you want some breakfast? I can make you some before I start."

"I'll get some at home," he told her. Deke kissed her neck, then he closed his eyes as he breathed in her scent, wishing he could bottle it and take the fragrance of her with him. How had he ever let himself get so involved with her? It was going to be hard to leave her today. He had plans to head to Vegas by late afternoon, and he still had to go by the Bar M. "You've been working hard, sweetheart. The place looks great."

Pleased that he'd noticed, she smiled at him. "You're surprised that I started cleaning my father's room, aren't you?" She'd spent the better part of yesterday, until Deke had arrived on her doorstep, stripping it of every reminder of the man whose love she'd never been able to obtain. All that remained to be cleared was one drawer full of junk and the shelf in his closet. "I've already packed most of his things. I was going to show you last night, but we sort of got sidetracked.'' She blushed, remembering that they'd only left her bed long enough to eat.

Deke glanced around the room, taking in the bare walls and the assortment of stacked boxes. His gaze went to the unmade bed, then shifted back to Mary Beth. He reached for her, but she put a firm hand to his chest, keeping him at a distance. ''Don't even think about it. I'm almost finished in here.''

He grinned, and despite her protest, kissed her hungrily. Her lips clung to his as he lifted his head. ''All right, sweetheart,'' he drawled, and he gave her a sexy grin. ''How about some help?''

She chuckled. ''Your timing's impeccable. All I have left is this drawer,'' she said, pulling it open. Nodding at the closet, she added, ''and that stuff on the shelf in the closet.''

He cocked his head and studied her. ''Has it been hard going through his things?''

''A little,'' she answered honestly. ''My father wasn't an easy man to understand. He rarely showed emotion. I accepted the fact that I could never do anything to please him a long time ago.'' Despite her words, a shiny tear formed in the corner of her eye.

Deke pulled her to him. ''I'm sorry he never appreciated you, Mary Beth.'' She was so beautiful, so sweet. Her father must have been crazy not to see how special she was. She sniffed, then turned toward the dresser and pulled out the drawer. Deke took it from her and put it on top of the dresser.

''Why don't you let me go through the rest of this?''

She shook her head. ''I'm okay,'' she said quietly, and she began fingering the items inside the drawer. ''Isn't it strange the things people keep.'' There was an assortment of odds and ends—an old wallet that she remembered her father carrying and a couple of his old watches. "Hmm, look at this."

Deke stepped closer and put his arm around her. He looked over her shoulder as she picked up a small, plain wooden box and turned toward him. "What is it?"

She studied it, her gaze perplexed. "I don't know." She lifted the lid. Inside was a silver key.

"What do you think it's for?" Deke asked.

Mary Beth stared at it, her eyes wide. "I've no idea. I've never seen it before."

"Did you find anything it would fit when you were going through the room?"

"No, nothing." Puzzled, she looked closely at it. "It doesn't have any markings or anything." Shrugging one shoulder, she added, "I doubt that it could open anything important."

Deke's curious gaze flicked to hers. "I don't know. Why would your father keep a key hidden in his drawer, if it didn't go to something he considered important?"

"You've got a point," she agreed. She turned to look around the room. "But I haven't seen anything—" Her gaze went to the closet. "What about up there?" she said, indicating the shelf in the closet.

"Let's have a look." They walked to the closet, and he began handing things down to her. Mary Beth took the items from Deke, then stuffed them in an empty box as he reached for more. "Wait, what's this?" At the very back of the shelf was a large silver box. He took it down and held it out to her.

Mary Beth's stomach knotted. "I wonder what's inside?"

"Try the key."

Biting her lip, she slipped the key into the small opening. It fit perfectly. Her fingers trembled as she turned it, then lifted the lid. "Oh, my God," she whispered, turning pale. "Deke, look." She barely got the words out before she took the box from him, then sank down on the edge of the bed. Her heart began to pound in her chest.

Deke sat on the bed beside her as he looked at the contents of the box. Inside was an array of mementos of Mary Beth's life—a picture of her as a baby, a locket of her hair pressed in a small square of wax paper, a barrette she'd worn as a child.

"Oh, Deke," she cried softly. "Look." She held up a blue ribbon. "I won this at the Texas State Fair when I was twelve. I remember coming home from school one day and finding it missing. I wondered where it had gotten to. I thought my mother had thrown it out." Sniffing back tears, she looked at Deke. "But she hadn't. My father had taken it, kept it hidden in here. All these years."

Deke rubbed her shoulder as she discovered a folded piece of paper. It was so old that it practically tore in the creases as she unfolded it. Inside was a drawing she'd made at a young age.

"I can't believe my father kept all this." Her throat tight, she could barely talk.

Tugging her closer, Deke touched his lips to her brow. He could only imagine what she was feeling. "Your father must have loved you in his own special way, sweetheart. Maybe he just couldn't say the words," he said solemnly.

"Maybe." Mary Beth couldn't remember a time when her father had ever said he loved her. He'd never shown much emotion toward her mother, either. Doubts assailed her. What if Deke was right? What if her father had loved her the only way he'd known how?

"He wouldn't have kept all this if he hadn't cared about you."

Mary Beth leaned against Deke, glad that he was there with her. "I never knew," she whispered shakily, thinking about all the times she'd tried to talk to her father. Her shoulders began to tremble as she clutched the box to her chest. "I thought... Deke, I thought he hated me."

Wrapping his arms around her, Deke held Mary Beth tight against him as she wept. He wished he had the power to ease her pain, but knew she had to work through her emotions concerning her father.

"I wasn't sorry when he died," she confessed breaking the silence that lay between them. Lifting her tear-streaked face, Mary Beth looked into Deke's eyes. She swallowed past the lump in her throat. "I wasn't grieving for him the day you made love to me. Not the way you and everyone else probably thought. My father was never around when we needed him. And when he was here, we didn't get along. I couldn't wait to grow up so I could leave here and get away from him."

Deke slipped the box from her hands and set it aside. Spotting some tissues, he grabbed a handful and gave them to her. "Don't feel guilty, Mary Beth."

"I can't help it. If I'd known—"

"But you didn't know. Don't tear yourself up over something you had no control over. Chances are that your father wouldn't have ever admitted his feelings even if you'd confronted him."

She sniffed and blew her nose. "You're right. I know you're right," she whispered sadly. She turned away to look at the box. Her eyes filled again.

And Deke held her while she cried.

Matthew McCall stood on the front porch of the large ranch house on the Bar M, and watched sharp streaks of lightning arc across the sky. The screen door opened behind him, and he looked at his uncle as he walked up beside him.

"Your mom sent me to tell you to get your butt inside," Deke said, leaning against one of the posts. "She doesn't think it's safe for you to be out here with the storm moving in." He had to agree with Catherine. It looked as if it was going to be a particularly bad one. Rain had been falling for the better part of the afternoon, and by the look of the darkening sky, it wasn't going to stop anytime soon. The local weather forecast had just confirmed his suspicions, calling for a severe line of thunderstorms to move through over the next few hours.

After doing some of Mary Beth's chores, Deke had finally headed for the Bar M when it began to rain. He'd planned to leave an hour ago for Las Vegas but had decided to wait until the storm passed.

The finals were due to start in two days. Deke had to get his mind off of Mary Beth and back on competing, if he stood a chance of winning. Still, as stupid as it sounded, he planned to stop by to see her again on his way out.

He looked off in the direction of her place. His eyes widened when he saw billows of thick black smoke rising in the sky. "What the hell?"

Startled, Matt glanced in the direction of his uncle's gaze. "Is that smoke?"

But Deke was already moving toward his truck, his fear for Mary Beth's safety ripping through his heart. "Get Ryder and Jake! Hurry!" he yelled over the roar of thunder. He jumped in his truck and started it. With a curse, he gunned the engine, then tore out of the yard.

Mary Beth jumped at the loud clap of thunder. A chill raced down her spine as a streak of lightning flashed outside her window and she heard a loud *crack!* That was close! She raced to the window and peered out, her heart beating wildly. Rain slashed against the ground so thick that she could barely see. Still, she couldn't shake the feeling that something was terribly wrong.

When Lightning and Lady began to bark, she hurried to the living room. Both dogs were in a frenzy at the front door. Grimacing, Mary Beth jerked it open and gasped.

The barn's on fire!

Flames shot toward the sky from the rafters of the barn. Giving little thought to her own safety, she rushed outside and ran across the yard. In seconds she was soaked to her skin, but she didn't care. Her hard work, what she'd struggled to build, was being torn from her. She fought against the wind and rain until she was able to unlatch the barn doors and pull them open.

"Stay!" she ordered the dogs when she realized they'd followed her. Taking a deep breath, she rushed inside the barn to free the horses. Already restless, they milled about in their stalls.

It wasn't until she'd released the first horse that she realized the seriousness of the fire. It had spread from the roof and now engulfed the sides of the old structure. She yelled and flapped her arms at the horse she was trying to free. His eyes wild, he finally raced toward the door. Shaking, she jerked her wet shirt out of her jeans, ripped it open, then held a part of it over her mouth and nose as she made her way to the next stall.

By the time she'd freed the last horse, the barn was completely consumed with smoke so thick she could barely breathe. With each step Mary Beth could feel herself becoming disoriented.

Oh, God! You have to get out now!

Then she heard Lightning and Lady. Barely able to see the door, she staggered in the direction of their persistent barks. Her lungs burned from the smoke, and she stumbled and nearly fell. Regaining her balance, she struggled a little farther, then dropped to her knees on the dirt just as she made it outside.

Choking, gasping for air, Mary Beth half crawled, half dragged herself away from the burning building as the rain beat down on her. Barking wildly, Lightning and Lady ran up to her, their cold noses sniffing her face. She hugged them to her, thankful that their barks had led her to safety. Struggling to her feet, she turned around. Then she screamed.

The fire had spread to the house. Despair overwhelmed her as all she could do was watch it burn. Flames licked up the side of it and engulfed the roof.

"No!" She darted forward, then stopped in her tracks. There was no way she could stop the fire. Not on her own.

Tears rolled down her cheeks. She was going to lose her home. Everything she'd worked so hard to achieve. Lost. She'd thought she hated this house and everything it represented. But she didn't.

The memory box!

Mary Beth bolted for the front door. She had to save it!

Eleven

Deke held Mary Beth's hand while she slept, concern etched on his brow.

She'd remained semiunconscious for the past two days. Her doctor had assured him that she should soon recover from her concussion. He wanted to believe that, but other than occasionally moving restlessly in her bed, Mary Beth hadn't shown any other signs of awakening.

His gaze slowly slid over her, lingering on her pale face. She looked so fragile. He sighed and lifted her hand to his cheek, pressing his lips to her palm. God, it was a miracle that she hadn't been burned. He sent up a prayer of thanks.

The afternoon of the fire, he'd arrived at Paradise to find the barn nearly burned to the ground and her house in flames—and Mary Beth nowhere in sight. Deke's worst fear, that she was still in the house, was confirmed when Lightning and Lady led him to the front door with anxious barks.

Barely able to see through the dense smoke, Deke had made his way inside and had seen Mary Beth struggling to make her way outside. But just as he'd reached her, a ceiling beam had fallen and struck her in the head. He'd felt his heart stop as she'd staggered, then collapsed to the floor.

At the sound of the door opening, Deke glanced up at Jake and Ryder walked into the sterile hospital room. His family had stayed with him at the hospital around the clock, lending support and ensuring that Mary Beth received the best of care. Deke didn't know what he would have done without them.

"How are you doing?" Jake asked Deke as he walked closer to the bed, his expression solemn as he looked at Mary Beth's still figure lying on the stark, white sheets.

"I'm okay." Deke's gaze never left Mary Beth.

"Has there been any change in her condition?"

Deke shook his head. He swallowed past the hard knot in his throat and squeezed her hand a little tighter.

Ryder walked over and put his hand on Deke's shoulder, then very cautiously said, "You know the finals start tomorrow. If you're gonna get there in time, you're going to have to leave soon."

"Dammit, I know what I have to do!" Letting go of Mary Beth, Deke got abruptly to his feet and shrugged Ryder's hand from his shoulder.

I hate you. The angry words he'd said to his father all those years ago ripped through his mind. Those hurtful words had tortured him for years. Now he was so close to fulfilling the promise that he'd made to his father. Only in order to participate in the finals, he would fail the one person he loved the most.

Mary Beth.

Jake and Ryder exchanged a look. "What was that all

about, Deke?'' Jake asked quietly, raising a dark brow. His youngest brother was the most easygoing of the three of them. Something had him wound tighter than a drum. When Deke remained silent, he said, ''C'mon, Deke, talk to us. We want to help you.''

Deke paced to the window, fighting against the urge to share his shame with his brothers. He wrestled with the decision another moment, then turned to look at them, his expression one of deep remorse.

''There's no easy way to say this,'' he began, jamming his hands in his pockets. ''You wouldn't remember any of this, Jake, because you were away at school the day Mom and Dad died in that plane crash.'' His voice was tight, his throat dry as he spoke. His gaze went to Ryder. ''Do you remember what happened the night before?''

Ryder looked thoughtful, then shook his head. ''I'm not sure what you're getting at,'' he said, his expression guarded. ''I remember that I was sick the night before with some kind of stomach flu or something. Mom had reconsidered going with Dad, but by morning I was feeling better.''

Deke didn't remember any of that. He only remembered the terribly crushing things he'd said to his father. ''I had a fight with Dad,'' he told them both, and his voice shook. He drew a deep breath, then forged on, ''I'd been giving him hell for a couple of months. Ignoring my homework. Skipping chores. Dad had restricted me from leaving the house.''

''That I remember,'' Ryder told him, thinking back.

''Yeah, well, I was hardheaded and snuck out, anyway.'' His eyes began to sting, and he blinked back tears. ''Dad discovered that I was gone, and he came after me, showing up at Becky Parson's house just as we were about to go out to the lake.'' Deke didn't have to explain *why* he and Becky were going to the lake.

''He dragged me home. I was embarrassed and angry. The entire ride back I wouldn't even speak to him.'' He gave a twisted smile. ''But you know Dad. He never could let anything go. He tried to talk to me, and we ended up having a huge fight.'' Deke gritted his teeth, then looked directly at his two brothers.

''I told him…God, I told him that I hated him.'' His face contorted with anguish. He paused as the memories slammed through his mind—the anger and pain, the hard silence that could never be broken. ''The next day, he and Mom were killed in that plane crash. I never got the chance to take back what I said,'' he admitted, his throat tight. ''I never got the chance to tell him I loved him.''

Jake looked confused. ''What does that have to do with the rodeo?''

''At his grave, I promised Dad that I'd win the championship for him.''

''And that's why you've pushed yourself so hard on the circuit?''

Deke nodded, his lips a thin, tight line.

Jake looked at Ryder, understanding dawning. Their father and Deke had shared a close relationship. Neither he nor Ryder had cared much for the rodeo, but Deke had loved going with their dad. Suddenly it all made sense. Deke had been killing himself for years, risking his life, to keep the promise he'd made.

To ease his conscience, to try and right the wrongs of his youth.

''I want to go,'' Deke admitted quietly. ''I think I have a good chance at winning this year, but—'' Closing his eyes, he drew in a deep breath, his heart aching inside his chest. His gaze went to Mary Beth, lying so still on the bed. How could he leave her? He couldn't stand the thought of her awakening and not finding him by her side.

Jake stepped a little closer. "You were just a kid, Deke. Dad knew you didn't mean what you said. He knew you loved him."

Fighting tears, Deke looked away. "I wish I could believe that."

Ryder gave Jake a nudge. "I think you'd better tell him."

Jake's brows wrinkled, his expression unsure. "I don't know."

Deke stared at them both. "Tell me what?"

"I can't think of a better time, Jake. Deke should know the truth. It'll help him to understand Dad, and to see that he's been unnecessarily torturing himself."

Jake nodded slowly, then his gaze went to Deke. "None of us is perfect, Deke. We all make mistakes, and we all need forgiveness at one time or another. I have, and so has Ryder. Dad was no exception."

"Yeah?" Deke sounded skeptical. He didn't see how anything Jake could say would ease his pain. His dad had been the perfect father, always there for them.

"Believe me when I say that I'm not telling you this to hurt you. I would never do that. I'm telling you so you'll understand that Dad would have been the first person to forgive you for what you said. Early on in his marriage to Mom, Dad had an affair." He glanced at Ryder, and with his look of encouragement, told Deke what he'd learned after their parents had been killed. "When I took over the ranch, I found some legal documents among Dad's things. He fathered me with another woman."

"What?" Stunned, Deke could hardly breathe.

"It's true," Ryder added. "I've seen the papers myself. Mom adopted Jake when he was just a few days old. We don't really know the story behind his birth, who his biological mother was or anything.''

"I know it's hard to believe." Jake touched Deke's shoulder.

"Sheesh." Deke looked into Jake's eyes. He'd never lied to him, so he knew that what he'd said was true. They were actually half brothers. It made sense, he thought, in an odd way. His oldest brother didn't look like the rest of them. He had brown eyes instead of blue, dark brown hair instead of blond. "How do you feel about this?" he asked, concerned.

"I let it bother me for a long time, but I've made peace with what Dad did. Mom had the heart to forgive him. Who was I not to? And she never treated me differently from the rest of you. I know she loved me," he said with sincerity. "Now you have to make peace with what happened between you and Dad that night. Because Dad loved you, no matter what you said to him.''

After all these years Deke realized that he'd beaten himself up over an anger that his dad would have understood. And in that moment he felt a huge weight lift from his shoulders. He hugged both of his brothers. Though he still wished he could have talked to his father before he'd died, he no longer felt the pressure to compete in the rodeo to prove his love for him.

"So, if you want to stay here with Mary Beth, do it with a free conscience," Jake said. He paused briefly, then added, "I know that you don't want to leave her. The thing is, I have a feeling that she'd be awfully furious if you missed the rodeo on her account.''

"I would be."

At the sound of Mary Beth's weak voice, all three men turned at once in the direction of the bed.

Deke was the first to react, and he hurried to her side.

"My God, sweetheart, you're awake!" he rasped, his heart pounding. He leaned over and smoothed her hair from her face.

Her eyes fluttered closed, then after a moment, opened lazily. She swallowed thickly, then focused her gaze on Deke.

Ryder quickly poured some water into a cup, added a straw, then handed it to Deke. He held it to Mary Beth's lips, and she took a small sip and swallowed. It was deliciously cool to her dry throat. "Thank you," she whispered. She glanced around the room, then frowned at the IV in her arm. "How long have I been here?" she asked, realizing that she was in the hospital.

"I'll let the nurses know she's awake," Jake said, turning toward the door.

Thinking that Deke and Mary Beth might want some privacy, Ryder walked around the bed. "I'll go with you."

"Two days," Deke told her, nodding at his brothers as they left the room. He took Mary Beth's hand in his, turned it over and kissed her palm. "How are you feeling?"

"My head hurts a little, but other than that, I feel okay."

"You have a mild concussion. A ceiling beam fell and hit you on the head. I've been worried sick about you. My whole family has been." He gave her a tender smile. "Most of them are in the waiting room. They'll probably bombard you any moment."

She blinked slowly. That explained the presence of his brothers in her room. "What was that about you not going to the rodeo?"

"I didn't want to leave you. I wanted to be here when you woke up."

"I'm awake now." She very carefully shook her head. "You can't miss the finals. You've worked so hard for this moment, Deke. And you have a real shot at winning. Besides, I'm fine.''

"Hush." He leaned down and briefly kissed her mouth. "We'll talk about it later.''

Nodding, she took another deep breath. "The dogs?''

"They're fine. They're at the Bar M.''

Relieved, she asked, "What happened to the house?''

"I'm sorry, sweetheart,'' he said with regret. "We couldn't save it." His brothers and the Bar M ranch hands had arrived on the scene right behind Deke. While he and Catherine had rushed Mary Beth to the hospital, they'd worked hard to put the fire out. But it had been too late to do anything except make sure it didn't spread.

Mary Beth's eyes watered. "No one was hurt?'' she asked on a gasp.

"No, everyone's okay.''

"Thank God,'' she murmured. She bit her lip. "I'm so sorry that you lost everything that you invested in Paradise, Deke.''

"Don't worry about it. The important thing is that you're all right.''

"I have insurance,'' she told him. "I was able to keep it up. So I'll be able to pay you back.''

"You're gonna need that money to rebuild.''

She wished that was true. But in her heart, there was only one reason for her to rebuild. If Deke loved her, if they had a future together, she'd stay in a heartbeat. But would they ever have a future together? Though he had stayed by her side at the hospital, it didn't mean that he loved her.

"There's no reason to start over again. You know I never planned to stay.'' She looked away, hardly able to stand the thought of leaving him.

"What?'' Deke stared at her in disbelief, his heart shattering. What was she talking about? Of course she was going to stay. He *wanted* her to stay. Dammit, she *had* to stay!

"I don't see any reason to rebuild, Deke. My goal was to make Paradise a success. With your investment, I was on the way to doing that. I've proved to myself that I could run the ranch. That's all I set out to do. I never had any long-term plans to stay."

Deke began to panic. He *had* to talk Mary Beth into staying. While he'd been waiting for her to awaken, he'd been busy making plans. He wanted a chance to show her that he loved her, wanted to spend the rest of his life with her. He couldn't let her leave.

Turning away, he grabbed her memory box that he'd kept with him at the hospital, thinking it was her connection to Paradise. "I managed to save this," he said quietly. "You had it in your arms when I carried you out of the house."

She blinked back tears. "Oh, Deke!" Lifting her hand, she ran her palm over the lid.

Leaning down close to her, he whispered, "Mary Beth, if you ever risk your life like that again, I swear I'll spank you." His kissed her lips, then gazed into her eyes. "You scared me half to death, sweetheart."

Looking appropriately chastised, she bit her lip. "I'm sorry. I guess I wasn't thinking. I just reacted." Her gaze inspected him, then went back to his face. "You're okay, aren't you?"

"I'm fine," Deke said, kissing her mouth again. This time he let his lips linger. He nipped her bottom lip with his teeth, then soothed it with his tongue.

Mary Beth moaned, then slid her arms around his neck and drew him closer. She loved him so much, her response to him was automatic. Her mouth opened in invitation, and he deepened the kiss. When he finally lifted his head, they were both breathing hard.

"Keep that up, and I'm gonna have to climb in that bed with you."

Blushing, she touched his face. Before she could say anything, the door opened and a crowd of people poured in and swarmed around her bed. Lynn and Russ Logan reached her first.

Lynn softly brushed the back of her hand against Mary Beth's cheek. "We were so worried about you, Mary Beth. You look flushed. How are you feeling?"

"I'm fine," Mary Beth assured her, knowing her warm cheeks had absolutely nothing to do with her injury. Jake, Catherine and Ryder came closer. Then Mary Beth saw Matthew. She smiled at him, and he winked at her.

"Thank you all for being here," she said, overwhelmed by their concern. She envied Deke his supportive and loving family.

"Let's give her some breathing space." Ryder nudged his sister out of the way to make room for the doctor.

An older gentleman with white hair and black-rimmed glasses appeared beside her bed. Mary Beth turned her head toward him.

"So, you are awake. Good. How do you feel?"

"Other than a slight headache, I feel fine," she assured him. She was anxious to get out of the hospital. Of course, she wasn't sure where she'd be going. She no longer had a home.

The doctor raised her bed, which lifted her into a sitting position. He asked her some questions, then made some notes on her chart. Everyone watched in silence as he flashed a light into her eyes and listened to her heartbeat with his stethoscope. Quietly chatting among themselves, they awaited his prognosis.

"I'd like to go home, please," Mary Beth said firmly. Then she realized what she'd said. "Well, I don't have a home, but I still want to leave."

The doctor looked up from her chart, his eyebrows raised. "Not too crazy about the accommodations, huh?" he asked, chuckling. "Now why doesn't that surprise me?" He looked at Deke when he spoke. "Well, I think it'd be safe for her to leave as long as someone can stay with her for a few days."

"Oh, but—"

"She'll be staying with us, doctor," Deke stated firmly. Her protest went unnoticed.

Mary Beth's eyes widened. "No, I—"

"Don't worry about a thing," Lynn added, her expression tender. "We'll take good care of her." She looked at Mary Beth. "Don't even try to talk us out of it. We've already set up a room for you at the Bar M. And the kids just love Lightning and Lady."

Mary Beth swallowed hard, forcing the knot in her throat down. She fought back the tears that filled her eyes. "That's very kind of you. All of you," she said, scanning their smiling faces.

Deke took her hand and squeezed it, his eyes full of tenderness. "You didn't think you'd be going anywhere else, did you?"

Mary Beth put the finishing touches on her makeup, then twisted and turned to check her reflection in her bedroom mirror. Her hair fell in glistening array around her shoulders, and the emerald-green dress she wore brought out the color of her eyes. She smiled at herself. It had been a long time since she'd enjoyed the Christmas holidays.

She hadn't expected to still be at the McCall ranch on Christmas morning, but that was exactly where she found herself. Deke and his family had welcomed her into their loving home, installed her in one of the bedrooms—the one next to Deke's—and made sure she was comfortable.

Upon the doctor's assurance that it was safe for her to travel, they'd whisked her away to Las Vegas once she'd left the hospital. Night after night, she'd watched with her heart in her throat as Deke competed for the bull-riding championship. On the last night, everyone in the stadium had erupted in hoots and whistles as Deke had taken first place and accepted his gold belt buckle.

Once they returned home, Mary Beth realized that Christmas was fast approaching. While in the past she'd merely tolerated the holidays, this year she truly possessed the spirit of Christmas. She treasured every moment of decorating the large McCall home along with Catherine and Ashley. Together, they draped garland along the mantel over the fireplace, hung a huge wreath on the front door and placed candles in the windows. The scent of bayberry drifted throughout the house.

Deke and his brothers hauled in a gigantic Christmas tree, and Mary Beth spent an entire afternoon helping the family decorate it with colored lights and an assortment of homemade ornaments. She had so much fun that she was almost disappointed when the task was done.

She and Deke made several trips to the mall, where she spent hours choosing just the right gift for each family member. Several times Deke had to drag her from the stores. She was so excited about her purchases that she would rush home to wrap each item and place it beneath the huge tree. She could barely contain her enthusiasm as she waited for Christmas to arrive, eager to see the delighted faces of the children as they opened their presents.

Being part of a family was a new and exciting experience for her. With each passing day, Mary Beth's love for

Deke only grew stronger. Caught up in the holiday spirit, she began to wish for the impossible—that Deke would fall in love with her.

"After all," she whispered to herself, "Christmas is the season of miracles."

Maybe she was being foolish, but her father's memory box had made her believe in miracles again.

Though Deke hadn't spoken words of love, that he desired her wasn't even questionable. Late at night, after everyone had gone to bed, he would sneak into her room and make love to her. He would have stayed with her all night had she not insisted that for propriety's sake he return to his own room before his family awoke and caught them in bed together. Deke assured her that his family knew *exactly* where he spent his nights. But early each morning he did as she requested and returned to his own bed.

Satisfied with her appearance on Christmas morning, Mary Beth left her room and headed for the den, anxious to join the McCalls as they gathered around the Christmas tree. Lynn and Russ and their son, Shayne, were just arriving as she came down the hall.

"Merry Christmas, Mary Beth," Lynn greeted her with her usual vibrant enthusiasm.

"Merry Christmas," Mary Beth replied with a heartfelt smile. She hugged Lynn, accepted a warm kiss on her cheek from Russ, then walked with them into the large den.

Deke looked up when Mary Beth entered the room, and his heart swelled as he watched her walk toward him. He'd been planning a big surprise for her for the past few weeks. Now that the time had arrived to give her his present, he was feeling anxious. Taking a deep breath to calm his nerves, he straightened from where he'd been kneeling on the floor and greeted her with a long kiss.

"Merry Christmas, sweetheart," he whispered against her mouth.

Mary Beth slid her arms around his waist, and smiled up at him. "Merry Christmas." It hadn't been that long ago that Deke had left her bed, sneaking out of her room just before daybreak. Mary Beth tilted her head as he nuzzled her neck.

"I have something special for you." He winked at her and planted a tender kiss on her lips.

"You already gave me something special this morning," she replied, her voice husky.

Deke groaned. Just thinking about making love to her earlier had him ready to drag her back to his bedroom. "Be good," he murmured thickly.

She giggled, then looked at the commotion around them. She'd never been happier than at that moment.

"Stop kissing and sit there, you two," Ashley said, pointing to one end of the enormous sofa. Deke immediately obeyed his sister-in-law, then tugged Mary Beth down beside him. She settled beneath the curve of his arm and rested her hand intimately on his thigh.

"This one's for you, Mary Beth," Ashley said with a smile as she passed her a gift from under the tree. Already opening their gifts from Santa, the twins, Michelle and Melissa, ignored everything around them. Ryder was sitting near them, holding Taylor in his arms.

"That's from us," Lynn said. She sat on the floor near the fireplace, holding her baby, Shayne. Russ was next to her, his arm around her shoulder.

"Thank you." Mary Beth grinned, then added the brightly wrapped package to the growing pile of gifts in front of her and Deke. She shivered with pleasure. She had a special gift for Deke and couldn't wait to give it to him.

Jake had seated himself comfortably at the opposite end of the sofa. Mary Beth laughed as he grabbed Catherine by the arm and pulled her down on his lap. Their son, Matthew, was busy helping the kids keep their gifts separated from the boxes and wrapping paper.

A flash caught Mary Beth's eye, and she glanced across the room. The colored lights from the tree were reflecting off Deke's championship bull-riding belt buckle, which was placed on the mantel. Mary Beth turned and looked at him, and her heart tripped over itself. She was so proud of him.

After the children finished opening their presents, things quieted down a bit and the adults took their turn. Mary Beth carefully opened each and every gift she'd received, anticipation building. An hour later there were piles of packages throughout the room. She'd received green silk pajamas from Lynn and Russ, a navy blouse from Jake and Catherine and a beautiful gold necklace from Ashley and Ryder. After thanking each of them, she gathered her packages together and carried them to her room where she'd left Deke's present.

Returning quickly to the den, she walked over and kissed him, then smiled as she handed him the gaily wrapped package.

Deke gave her an amused grin. "For me?"

Mary Beth nodded, then touched his arm, drawing his gaze to hers. "I hope you like it," she said softly. At the time, she'd thought it would be the perfect gift. Now she wasn't so sure. Her gaze sought Lynn's, and Deke's sister smiled brightly and gave her an encouraging nod. "It was my idea," Mary Beth confessed, feeling suddenly nervous, "but Lynn helped me with it."

The room grew quiet as Deke tore off the red ribbon and removed the candy-cane wrapping paper. He opened the lid of the box, then spread open the tissue paper. Inside was a photograph of himself with his father. Beautifully framed in silver and gold. It had been taken at the first rodeo Deke had competed in. He studied it almost reverently, then turned toward Mary Beth.

"I can't believe you thought of this," he said, gazing at her with disbelief. "I love it." His throat closed with heartfelt emotion. With his family watching, he whispered thank you against her lips.

"I'm glad you like it," she said, kissing him back.

"I've got something for you, too." He signaled to Matthew, who'd been waiting for his cue.

Her curiosity piqued, Mary Beth watched as Deke's entire family gathered to stand behind the sofa. She heard Matthew whistle sharply, then she laughed as Lightning and Lady trotted into the room, Santa hats perched on their heads.

Lightning held a small, red paper bag between his teeth. He came up to Mary Beth and stopped in front of her, his big eyes staring up at her. Beside him, Lady barked and nudged Mary Beth's hand. Laughter erupted throughout the room as she took the bag from Lightning. Still chuckling, she looked at Deke. "That was too cute," she said brightly, as Matthew called the dogs away. Then she opened the bag.

A tingle raced down her spine. Inside the bag was a tiny, blue velvet box. Her eyes flashed to Deke's, and his gaze held hers. He went down on one knee. Stunned, Mary Beth stared at him, her eyes wide.

"Mary Beth. I love you with all my heart. Will you marry me?"

Mary Beth's mouth dropped open. Her mind whirled in

a hundred different directions. Struggling, hardly able to breathe, she found her voice. "Oh, my. Oh, Deke." Tears gathered in the corners of her eyes, then quickly spilled down her cheeks. "You want to *marry* me?"

The suspense practically killing him, he stood and took the small box from her, opened it and withdrew a sparkling diamond. "Oh, yeah, sweetheart, I really do." If his heart hadn't been beating so wildly, he might have laughed at the picture she made. He couldn't understand her surprise. Surely she must have realized that he was in love with her.

An enormous smile burst on her face, love for him shining in her eyes. "Yes!" she whispered fiercely, her heart beating wildly. "Oh, I love you, Deke." She threw herself in his arms and kissed him hard.

Deke deepened the kiss, feeling as if he could devour her right then and there. Whoops and whistles erupted from behind them. Deke tore his mouth from Mary Beth's, and his family watched as he slipped the ring on her finger.

Vaguely aware that Deke's family had begun to retreat from the room, Mary Beth swiped tears from her cheeks with the back of her hand. She looked into Deke's eyes. "I have loved you, Deke McCall, nearly all of my life," she confessed, and she slid her arms around his waist. "I know I told you that I'd had a crush on you, but the truth is, I fell in love with you when I was in my teens. And I never stopped loving you."

Deke smiled at her, mesmerized by the glow in her eyes. "I didn't know," he whispered, overwhelmed by her confession.

"I'd always secretly hoped that you would notice me, but I never let myself believe that you would ever fall in love with me." She sniffed, then blinked back more tears. "I moved to San Antonio to try to forget you, but I couldn't. When you made love to me after my father died, I knew in my heart that I would always love you.''

"I'm sorry I hurt you when I walked away from you," Deke said. "But when I made love to you, I knew I was in trouble." He took her hand and held it against his chest. "You touched my heart. I had to leave you because I didn't want to hurt you like I'd hurt my father."

Mary Beth understood that now. Deke had told her about his father's affair and how Jake had helped him to find peace within himself. "I know." She clung to him, her eyes drifting shut as he took her mouth, his tongue sweeping inside and touching hers. She moaned softly when he lifted his lips.

"There's one more thing," Deke said, holding her tight against him. "I want you to know that wherever you want to call home, I'm willing to go."

A little confused, she tilted her head. "What? What are you saying?"

"You had all those travel magazines, and you said at the hospital that you didn't want to rebuild Paradise. Although I think that would be the perfect place for us to live, I'll be happy anywhere you want to go as long as I have you by my side."

"Oh, Deke," she murmured, and her heart slammed against her chest. "I thought I didn't want to live here because of all the unhappy memories of my childhood. But I can't think of a better place for you and me to start our life together than on Paradise. I don't want to leave here, *ever,*" she whispered fiercely.

"I love you so much." Her heart swelling with love, Mary Beth hugged him to her. She'd received her Christmas wish, after all.

Deke was her miracle.

Epilogue

As she stood at the front door of her newly built home, Mary Beth watched Deke's truck come to a stop in front of the house. He got out, and her heart gave that special little thump that she always felt when she looked at her husband. She stepped outside and waited on the porch to greet him. "There's Daddy now," she whispered to the three-month-old baby in her arms.

Kissing the baby's soft cheek, Mary Beth sighed with contentment. It seemed there was no end to the miracles in her life. So much had happened during the past year, it hardly seemed possible that she and Deke were just celebrating their first anniversary. Neither of them had wanted to wait to get married, so with the help of Deke's family, they'd quickly put together a wedding and had been married on New Year's Day.

Upon hearing the truck door slam, Lightning and Lady had bounded out of the barn and were now racing straight for Deke. Mary Beth chuckled at their antics as they pranced around his legs, begging for attention. He gave both dogs a pat, then looked up at her as he reached the steps.

"Hey, beautiful."

Her heart swelling, Mary Beth lifted her lips to his. Oh, how she loved this man. She closed her eyes and breathed in his scent as he kissed her, savoring the taste of him.

"Hi," she said, when their lips parted.

"I'm sorry we had to cancel tonight," he told her with genuine regret. "I'll make it up to you next weekend." They'd changed their dinner plans when Lynn had called earlier that afternoon. Her baby, Shayne, was sick with an ear infection and she couldn't leave him, and Russ had needed Deke's help caring for an injured horse.

"We're together, that's what counts." She tilted her head and smiled at him. "Come inside. I'll put Andrea down while you clean up."

Deke took the baby from her, pressed a kiss to his daughter's velvety reddish-blond hair, then followed Mary Beth into the house. Andrea Nicole McCall stared at him with wide, innocent eyes.

He stopped in his tracks as they entered the dining room, then turned a startled gaze on Mary Beth. "How'd you put this together?" he asked, surprised that she'd had enough time to plan a romantic candlelight dinner in the time he'd been gone. He sniffed and smelled the enticing aroma of basil, tomatoes and warm bread. "Lasagna?" he asked, his eyes lighting up.

She chuckled. "Your favorite meal."

He handed her the baby. "I'm starved," he said, then he kissed his wife. When the kiss began to grow into more, she gently moved out of his arms. "Dinner first."

Deke groaned, then hurried out of the room to shower.

Mary Beth went to the nursery and put Andrea to bed. She stood at the crib and stared down at her little girl. Never in her life would Mary Beth have ever believed that living on Paradise would be so fulfilling, so absolutely perfect. After a week of honeymooning at a remote resort in Mexico, they'd returned home to begin rebuilding the house. Soon after construction started, they'd discovered she was pregnant.

Not totally a surprise, since they'd talked and decided to start a family right away. At first Mary Beth had been hesitant, wondering if Deke was truly finished competing in the rodeo. But he had assured her that since he'd fallen in love with her, he was happier than he'd ever been in his life. He'd convinced her he was ready to put down roots right here, become a rancher and start a family. It had been a race to see if they could finish the house before the baby arrived. They had, but just barely.

She heard the shower go off. Turning out the light she went into the bedroom, walking inside just as Deke was buttoning his shirt. Desire stirred deep inside her at the sight of him. Walking over to him, she slipped her arms around him, aligning herself against his back.

Deke turned in her arms and pulled her to him. "I love you," he whispered huskily, then his mouth took hers in a hungry kiss. Mary Beth clung to him, her body responding to the warmth of his. "I thought you wanted to eat," he remarked, his eyes teasing as he lifted his lips.

"I do. Come on." Arm in arm, they walked to the kitchen. Together they carried the food into the dining room and placed it on the table. Mary Beth smiled up at Deke as he held her chair, then waited as he took his seat and opened the chilled red wine. He filled two glasses and handed her one before taking his own.

"I never dreamed I could be this happy," she said softly as she looked at him, her eyes misting.

Deke looked into her eyes. "I didn't, either, sweetheart." His heart throbbed almost painfully. But it was a good kind of ache. He cherished this woman and their beautiful daughter. After his father's death, Deke hadn't thought he deserved love. But through Mary Beth, he'd learned that true love was unconditional.

He leaned toward her, and she met him halfway, their lips touching briefly, then again, longer, clinging momentarily until he finally drew away and gazed into her eyes.

He was going to love this woman for the rest of his life.

* * * * *

In December 2002

SILHOUETTE *Romance*®

presents the next book in
Diana Palmer's
captivating *Long, Tall Texans* series:

LIONHEARTED

Leo Hart had no intention of falling prey to any woman—
especially not a debutante-turned-cowgirl like Janie Brewster.
But all of Jacobsville knew Janie was on a mission to lasso
the irresistible cattleman—even if it meant baking biscuits
and learning to rope cattle! Will Janie succeed in making
the last Hart bachelor a bachelor no more…?

**Don't miss this stirring tale from international
bestselling author Diana Palmer!**

Available only from Silhouette Romance at your favorite retail outlet.

Silhouette®

Where love comes alive™

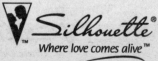

COMING NEXT MONTH

#1483 THE PLAYBOY & PLAIN JANE—Leanne Banks
Dynasties: The Barones
Gail Fenton was immediately attracted to her boss, gorgeous
Nicholas Barone, but she assumed he was out of her league. Then
suddenly Nicholas seemed to take a much more *personal* interest in her.
Was she wrong, or had this Cinderella finally found her prince?

#1484 BECKETT'S CONVENIENT BRIDE—Dixie Browning
Beckett's Fortune
While recovering from an injury, police detective Carson Beckett tracked
down Kit Chandler Dixon in order to repay an old family debt. But he got
more than he bargained for: beautiful Kit had witnessed a murder, and
now she was in danger. As he fought to keep her safe, Beckett realized
he, too, was in danger—of falling head over heels for sassy Kit....

#1485 THE SHEIKH'S BIDDING—Kristi Gold
The Bridal Bid
Andrea Hamilton and Sheikh Samir Yaman hadn't seen one another for
years, but one look and Andrea knew the undeniable chemistry was still
there. Samir needed a place to stay, and Andrea had room at her farm. But
opening her home—and heart—to Samir could prove very perilous
indeed, especially now that she had their son to consider.

#1486 THE RANCHER, THE BABY & THE NANNY—Sara Orwig
Stallion Pass
After he was given custody of his baby niece, daredevil Wyatt Sawyer
hired Grace Talmadge as a nanny. Being in close quarters with
conservative-but-sexy-as-sin Grace was driving Wyatt crazy. He didn't
want to fight the attraction raging between them, but could he convince
Grace to take a chance on love with a wild cowboy like himself?

#1487 QUADE: THE IRRESISTIBLE ONE—Bronwyn Jameson
Chantal Goodwin knew she was in trouble the minute Cameron Quade,
the object of her first teenage crush, strolled back into town. Quade was
the same, only sexier, and after what was supposed to be a one-night
stand, Chantal found herself yearning for something much more
permanent!

#1488 THE HEART OF A COWBOY—Charlene Sands
Case Jarrett was determined to honor his late brother's request to watch
out for his widow and unborn child. The truth was, he'd secretly loved
Sarah Jarrett for years. But there was a problem: She didn't trust him.
Case knew Sarah *wanted* him, but he had to prove to her that her fragile
heart was safe in his hands.

SDCNM1202